A WHITE ROMANCE

Virginia Hamilton

PHILOMEL BOOKS
New York

First Impression

Library of Congress Cataloging-in-Publication Data
Hamilton, Virginia.   A white romance.
Summary: As her all-black high school becomes more racially mixed,
Talley befriends a white girl, who shares her passion for running,
and becomes romantically involved with a drug dealer.
[1. Race relations—Fiction.   2. Friendship—Fiction.
3. Afro-Americans—Fiction]   I. Title. PZ7.H1828Wh   1987   [Fic]   87-2400
ISBN 0-399-21213-2

To Jaime Levi and Leigh Hamilton Adoff.

To Chris Motter, heavy rock bass player who said, while hearing pop music on the radio: "I'd rather listen to nothing really loud."

Grateful acknowledgment to Jaime Levi for his expert aid with the book's concert scene. He gave generously of his splendid eye for detail in the depiction of typical happenings at arena rock concerts.

A WHITE ROMANCE

Chapter
ONE

"**B**ook, girl! Move it!" Talley told herself. She sat on the stoop, unable to push herself yet. "Run!" In her head, she ran in long easy strides through nearly empty streets. The thought of muscles flexing and the smooth system of her insides as she ran made her throat thicken. Feel like crying, sometimes, too, when I'm running, she thought.

Running was as simple as breathing for her. Her habit was to imagine the whole route before she actually moved herself to run. In a minute, she would be on her way to pick up her girlfriend Didi and go on about their business back over to Didi's house. She was still in her sweats; homework was in the red bookbag dangling down from one shoulder. The bag wasn't heavy.

"Didi, girl, I feel so good today! Too-dawn-cool, give it up for one more hour, girl." "*It*" meaning Roady, Didi's main dude.

"I got to get over quick, see about Roady," Didi'd said. "You come on by soon as you can."

Talley was just about ready to get into her form to run

out the day. Instead, she sat awhile, unmoving, thinking about Didi's main boy. Roady. She could think over a whole semester while preparing herself to go over to Roady's house.

Far's I'm concerned, dude's got some seriously scrambled brains, Talley thought. Part I can't stand about picking up Didi is riding up Roady's ugly, dirty building. Scare me to death! So what if they looking out for me to come? They don't ride up with me. And I still have to run down the town by myself.

She would take a bus partway. There were streets she wouldn't run down.

Ugly low-storied apartment houses. In her head she was able to empty out the streets of menace, and sprint by the places. Some had their windows closed up with metal sheets. They seemed to stare blankly at her. This was near where the freeway came snaking around. It went right over some of the sheeted houses.

Across the highway was a rubber-tire plant that was death-still and quiet. Its gates were padlocked shut. Talley had seen it so many times, she could picture it in detail. All its formerly employed were now the downtrodden, the downgraded and the downcast. Most of them were on the hated, the dreaded "handout," they called it. They despised themselves for giving in to hunger and taking The Welfare. Or maybe they had drifted away to other big cities.

She shivered, not wanting her Poppy to ever become one of them. That brought her Poppy clear to mind again. There didn't seem to be a moment in her life when her dad didn't enter her head to mess things up. But she knew she mattered to him and, she had to admit, he mattered to her.

Poppy sure wouldn't want me bookin' out to where Roady live, she thought.

She dug her running shoe into the cracked sidewalk in front of her. She pictured the broken sidewalk along a fairly empty thoroughfare where she must run. That highway snaking through the city was wide and black. If anyone was going to block her path, try to mug her, it would happen there. Out there, the sky above her would look gray-purple. And by the time she got there, it would most likely start to rain. She could *perform* in rain. She ran almost truer when it rained. Maybe it was that she was more conscious of slippery surfaces and compensated.

Just don't give me some snow out there. Please.

This whole town is blackout city. Going to go to its grave in a blackoutmobile. What's one like, a blackoutmobile? Big as the night, I bet, but all wavery-velvet. Spread out, like you spread out a newspaper. It will shrivel around the edges, burning, but you can't see the fire. Just the black shriveling up.

Look at these sidewalks. In her head, seeing: look at everything so empty.

Each evening on that dying side of town, her best friend, Didi, was up in a world with Roady Dean Lewis. If Talley Barbour wanted to see Didi Adair, she had to go get her friend and bring her on out of there. Like, pulling her right out of Roady Dean's head. Talley could do it, too.

Only me, put some sense in the child's brain long enough to get her home and in shape for tomorrow's nerds and freak-faces, and dweebs and chills. Me.

Didi didn't worry about parents. She only had one now, just like Talley. Parents were a screech-and-halt.

Wrecks, almost, always worn-out exhausted or on the verge of flare-outs. Talley's dad could be like that. But Didi's mama was different, most of the time.

She know exactly what's on my mind, Talley thought. Knows everything. Except about Didi, her own kid.

Somehow, stopping over Roady's to pick up Didi all the time kept Talley from breaking down. Lone-city. And it was what kept her friend on the right side of some serious mess. Her mom can't do nothing with her. Don't even know she can't, Talley went on, thinking.

Running smoothly, even strides, right out from the gutter along the street. That's what she would do in a minute. The sound of her own breath would be all she would hear. Feel the coolness of day-ending on her face. Feeling glad she couldn't see the shine her sweat made. She hoped nobody would come along her way and see how she had such sweaty skin when she ran.

Her mama don't know what Didi's into in the first place. Wish I didn't know, either, Talley thought. Poppy see me one time, I'm going to catch the flare. Maybe he have me transferred out of Colonel Glenn too. He don't like it's a magnet deal with all be-white coming in cars and new be-black coming in from all over town. They all weird, and druggies, he says.

It's not true. Shoot. You have some of every kind in a place the Magnet's size. And I don't see what so good about the down-and-out I grew up with here. Just 'cause they go to our church.

Her Poppy wouldn't get home until twelve, working the four-o'clock shift. She had been upstairs in their apartment for no more than thirty-five minutes. Got her sandwich and milk. Had a candy bar. Took a few minutes to make her and her dad's bed. Cut back out. Nothing to do up there but study.

Didi won't study even if you paid her. How come some kids got natural brains and don't care, either? Didi'll pretend so she'll look like me and everybody else. I mean, if she want to, girl can open a book and close it and know everything in it that fast. Now I'm smarter than lots of *them*. So it's not just because she be-white. Funny, how you don't think about her so pale and me be-brown-reddy until the no-counts knock into you, accidentally-on-purpose. She just not into school all the time. She into Roady Dean Lewis.

Talley sighed, feeling sad, all of a sudden. She got up with ease and started walking. She was little, yet she was smooth, lithe and lean. She seemed to be coiled somewhere inside. Not tightly, but neatly coiled, ready to let loose power anytime she needed it. Her emotion was right there next to the coil. It was a perfect springboard. Her form would stand before she ever knew it would. Her feelings would rise with her springy bounce, would leap to her heart in a thrill of aching sorrow or love.

We can go along, go along, she thought. Her mind made its own leaps the same way, from one group of thoughts to another. Easy as walking, her mind-leaps were.

After a long time of going along just as smooth, something have to cause it, she thought. Some problem in school. Somebody say some name-calling, some real mess come down. It be there that quick, right up in our faces.

She sighed. I'm tired of the jitters.

She came out of her head suddenly and started running for real. Didn't know she was going to book out. Her sweet insides knew. Her legs, arms started. Her body gathered itself in strength, the way air lifted and shaped a balloon.

13

She was on her feet. And man, she was running!

A White Romance was there in the calm part of her insides. AWR. In her memory as she ran.

Like a flower growing and growing, she thought.

It might've happened yesterday, so clear was the memory. But it did happen six months ago. September. Did lilies bloom in the fall? AWR started with the pale kids drawn by the Magnet to her ordinary be-black school.

"Be cool, be-school! Inner sit-tay," was the way the *home* boys and babies said it. "The get-toh." Their inner-city wasn't what they would call a ghetto. They called their area The Neighborhood. *"Hey, Home, see you got some new threads. You making all the money. It all over The Neighborhood. Know what you into. You in the army. You cool, Jim. You making it all. Don't mess up!"*

It wasn't any real bad scene in their neighborhood, outside of some druggies and prostitutes. Just a few. But some bad stuff was everywhere. Hang-tail, stupid, sickly crackheads. A few sick-looking men and ladies, dealing.

It was just that the mostly steady working folks couldn't pick up nothing. Plants closed, hoping to re-open on the fringes of town. They still had their skeleton work crews. Stores closed and closing in The Neighborhood. You couldn't buy much; but then, you didn't have much to buy *with*. Everybody living next door to down-and-out, so to speak. Somebody not living any better than someone else, but trying to.

Everybody having a time getting it on. That was what The Neighborhood called *ache-o-nomics*. Hungry-nomics. So they hung tough, forever, some, if they had to. Black-o-nomics. Her Poppy's night-watchman job for three plants was a handle hold, he'd had it so long. He got to ride his rounds in a company car, too. He carried a cop radio and a cop gun. Poppy made Talley safe; she loved him for it.

The Homes didn't like their school taken over by be-white. "Why *they* comin' to *our* school? When civil rights come back?" Asking teachers, the AP, everybody. "Why come *they* can't make *they* school a Magnet and we go to *they* neighborhood?"

Home boy knew the answer to that. Shoot. He'd quit in another year, anyway. Join the Air Force, if he could. Mostly, he'd hang still as long as he could. Get into nothing. Get him some nowhere and no trouble.

You had the separate blocks in the city; you had the downtown with businesses, streetcars and buses. You also had the high-crime areas, everything any city had, Talley was thinking. Running, she had a sudden, swift cramp in her hamstring. She broke stride, limped a moment, but kept running. Massaging it as she went.

Cars. Everybody coming in from *their* neighborhoods, working in offices.

Some of us working in the offices, too. Lots of us do. You have to admit, some us got some jobs.

She felt that she could get one if Poppy only would let her. But she was scared. It was hard, leaving The Neighborhood. She left it only when she went to Roady's. Usually once a day, if she wanted to help out Didi.

You have some gangs but Poppy says they mostly confined to the East Side of town. Not the Magnet, not The Neighborhood. But more near the big industrials farther out on the way to the suburbs.

She had been out there to the suburbs—Fairwood and Oaklawn. She used to play soccer out there before she had to quit. Who needed it? Be-white, mostly. Some Veet-nams, they called all Asians. And the mixed on the fringes, where Didi came from. You always had some

15

mixed, mostly be-black and be-white, even in The Neigh-borhood. Talley didn't have to worry about none of them. Didn't think about them, even.

Some fine houses, though, out there in the suburbs. Really big places with lawns like soccer fields. Leave it to Roady to give it all up.

Shoot, Talley thought. Roady, none of us into wealth. Let 'em have it.

She was running true. Her lungs expanded like a mother of a machine.

She and all The Neighborhood had this great big school. That's how come it could be turned into a mag-net. The Colonel Glenn had a capacity, three thousand, and full. They had made it into a magnet, Poppy told her, because they had the Black Elected Officials who could get things done in the state legislature. That's why you had to keep The Neighborhood. By the time Talley was three years old, she knew what block voting was. Her Poppy might be a night watchman, but he knew to teach her all that had been, was, and still was. Wasn't a lot of be-black kids in The Neighborhood knew all the things her Poppy taught her.

The church folks like her Poppy usually were the ones who knew things. They didn't let everything get them down. They stayed together close. Walking together, staying together, children. They were into marrying and burying and working nine to five and overtime. They had to hustle on the side, some, but who didn't in be-black-onomics? So what if she didn't believe half of what her Poppy said?

Keep everything the same, keep integration out—that's what her Poppy and most folks wanted in The Neighborhood.

And they wrong as they can be, Talley thought. We still

in the inner sit-tay. We make it so we stay put and allow *them* to come in on *us*, too. They come and go and see as they please. We don't move, we don't learn a thing.

But it was there, A White Romance, AWR, like a part of her network, her screen of pretty pictures, a bloom of some kind. It sat there in the O's of figure-eights to smooth highways through spring-green hills and mountains. Pretty little cabins all in the flowering woods. Talley kept such pretties in clear pictures inside her. She kept AWR in manicured lawns—long skirts and pink parasols. And safely away from all the messes you could come across in these "sit-tay" streets.

Abruptly, she stopped her mind-glide toward AWR. She wasn't ready yet. She had to sweep the streets and Roady's building clean. Roady and Didi, first.

Chapter

TWO

Thought I heard somebody behind . . . nobody behind me. Girl, get inside before it's evening, and you'll be fine. Get on the bus now.

Talley went two blocks farther and waited for the right city bus. It came after about six minutes. It was half-full of students from practices out of school, or jobs. Some middle-age women. Nothing to worry about. Guys always stared at her. They made her feel dumb. She closed her eyes and rode out the ride.

Lucky! Off the bus, she was sprinting out along the curb. Lucky to be by myself. Safe. But I should watch it. Swear, one of these times, I'm going to get into trouble out here by myself. This the time of day when everybody inside, watching television. Getting home, if they someplace else.

She knew she could always run away from somebody approaching her. She could outrun most dudes. And if they were track guys, they wouldn't want to hurt her. She wouldn't need to outrun them.

Is that true? A tiny voice inside questioned whether

18

trouble was as easy to get rid of as that. Or if trouble gave you a chance to book. But it was such a small, weak sound. She brushed it off like a piece of lint.

She was close now and she ran the rest of the way hard, to hit the high. She reached the aerobic when she felt her skin tingling all over. The tingling heat came flowing down, like the sweetest and tartest icy-cold lemonade you could spill down your throat on the hottest summer day. She figured it was the way it felt when you were high on some stuff.

Always freer in her head than she was for real. She didn't need any real stuff. Give her her legs; let her run. No matter that her legs were short; her thighs, short, power muscles. They could conquer, Jim. She, a stone runner. So was Didi, and Didi, tall blond and a fox. Long legs, long muscles. But Didi couldn't outrun short, be-proud, be-black Talley Priscilla Barbour.

Always. Been on my mind since I met her.

Thoughts, lifted out of Talley's head like the heat from running.

Never let her beat me—why? Because you can't, that's all, long as she whuh and you bluh. Ha-ha. Whuh and bluh, that's funny.

You know that's wrong, that's no good.

Poppy would say, "Right, young lady. If they white and bust in on your territory, you always got to beat them."

Why can't he say "young woman?" He never will call me "young woman," but "young lady." And he's wrong as he can be. Tell him sometime. You got to make a conscious effort, Poppy. Else nothing's never going to change. The Neighborhood never going to reach up unless you reach up and out yourself. I got to stop saying "girl," too.

But that kind of stuff that her Poppy believed was what

19

all The Neighborhood was into, she knew. Talley could see the crowd at a soccer meet as clear as day. All the stands full of parents and little kids. Popcorn and soft drinks, and if it's still cold, they have coffee. Students, standing and shouting; she could catch a few words when she felt like turning the wind down in her ears to listen, "Beat her, Talley! School, nuthin! Team, nuthin! You b-b, you beat that b-w!" Talking about the chicks on the all be-white team that had come to play them.

B-b was the code, the jive. Everybody knew it was be-black, even those be-white.

They brought their own drill team and marching band, Jim. We got dazzled by their uniforms and matching sweats. They got oveh on us.

Didi and me on the same team, and they yelling like that. So wrong! Didi and me want to win for the school. We couldn't take that mess so we cut out of the team. They want us for track but we won't. Oh, we fool around the track, running each other. I'm that much faster. But she's smart. She learns so fast, Jim. She could beat me if she wanted to. Maybe. Not so sure about that.

But it won't matter because she doesn't care to beat me. She wants to run just like I do. She gives hard enough keep my pace and to come in second behind me. She's living on cream puffs, bottles of milk. Most the time, she have cantaloupe or fruit cup and tea for lunch, if she can't find a beer. Child is wild. And she still can come in second! Shoot.

That's the way it was with Didi. She didn't study, didn't need to because she could read something once and know it cold. Lived on air. You had to watch her for two days before you ever saw her inhale a hundred calories. Roady was like that, too. Knew everything and cared about nothing but music and Didi, if he cared about her.

And didn't eat for days. Just drink and . . . taking stuff, whatever it was he kept in the little box. Talley didn't want to know.

"Don't know can't hurt you," Poppy say.

Always, thinking about Poppy and then, AWR on a day like today when she felt all by herself made her want to cry.

I wish just once to have —. That was her most secret thought. Other girls have them. So am I ugly? I wish just once —. She threw out the idea into the flow of wind and sweat. . . . *to have a boy* — It sailed into the air. . . . *likes me.* It was gone where she couldn't tell.

"Well, here we are," she said, out loud. She was there, walking up to the door. Just five steps up and you are there. She went up on tiptoes, counting, "One, two, three, four, five." She gave her hips a little twist with each step.

The building was one of those heavy, brown-brick places near industrials. Cars lined up on either side of the street. You never saw too many people. Some old people, walking slowly. They usually went out, five and six together. They talked loud. They had whistles dangling around their necks. Other side of the street. Talley heard them shuffling out from a building, on their way somewhere where Seniors might go. "Why don't they stay in this time of day?" she said to the door.

"Who's 'they'?" someone answered her.

Talley clamped her mouth shut. Guy, standing in the doorway of the building. She'd been looking at her feet and speaking to herself. Then, the Seniors had distracted her.

"Huh?" she said. "Um, didn't see you." Flooded with embarrassment, she felt she would go through the cement steps. I am so dumb, talking out loud! She fumbled, opening the outer door. Without moving much, the guy stuck out his arm and held the door for her above her head.

"You talk to yourself like that all the time?" he said.

Should she look at him? She thought fleetingly, Poppy say always look your assailant in the eye. Let him know you know what he's wearing, how tall he is, so you can identify him. Fear creeped in her heart. She didn't dare believe this was it, to get hurt. She was too scared to look at him. "Thanks," she mumbled, ducking under his arm through the open door. She got a whiff of warm breath and after-shave. Blow hair, cut long, baby soft brown. The be-white boys sure enough loved that after-shave. Couldn't smell their rank selves at all. After-shave stank up the whole school.

She spun around. He was still holding the door. "Hey! I've seen you, at Colonel Glenn," she said.

"Bingo! Yeah, sweets . . ." he murmured. He did a complete turn-around and he was inside with her, the door easing closed behind his back. Some air of aggression about him in his studded leather jacket, although he hadn't made a move on her. Hands in his pockets. Lean but strong, built for speed. "I seen you before, too." Looking down at her, not smiling. Something light in his eyes, maybe dangerous.

"You . . . you live in Roady Dean's building?" *Don't turn your back on him!* But how are you going to get through the inside doors? Ring the buzzer. Callin' me sweets. Didi will buzz back. You push the door, it opens. *Don't turn your back . . .*

"You lose," he was saying. "Roady lives in *my* building. And anyhow, whatcha doing outside the ghetto?"

She could tell he was teasing but he made her mad all the same. She reached over to the buzzer panel and rang the third little button down. "I don't live in any ghetto," she said, very dignified. "*You* folks always have to think *we* live *strange*." She teased him back, made him smile. "I live in The Neighborhood. I go wherever I want, it's a free country. Wouldn't live out here for nuh-thang."

He grinned at her. "Ahhh, little Ms. Mouth," he said, shaking his head, looking her up and down. Well, it was true, she could talk herself out of most scenes. Guys really could seem to attack you with their eyes. But there was no law against looking. Everybody scoped on everybody else. Nobody took the be-white to heart. "I seen you running with Didi. Little Miz Roxanne." He laughed.

Don't you call me that! "My name's Talley," she said, hotly. "And you wrong, too, yourself. Didi running with *me*."

The door buzzer sounded, cutting through her anger. She leaned on the door and it opened. Keeping her hand on it until it almost closed, she whispered at him in her most syrupy voice, eyes flashing, "If you lived here, whyn't you open the do' fo' me?" Putting it on. She saw the look in his eyes. It made something flash-hot within her lean toward him. The same heat came from him, searing her. It happened so quickly, the feeling and the lean. It took her breath that fast, and was gone.

She was on the inside now, before he could answer. He was still on the outside of the inner locked doors. He lifted his hand with his keys, grinning.

So he lives here. What's wrong with you? Nobody's going to mess up in their own house. Get on the elevator.

He hadn't made a move. She turned her back as nonchalantly as she could. The elevator sat there, waiting for her.

Lucky!

She got in, pushed the button. The dude was still here, watching.

Watched me walk here. Think he's something and he's not good for nothing!

She could see him grinning. She heard him call, "So long, Talley!"

He had got her name out of her; she hadn't thought to find out his.

Well, who cares!

But it made her mad to have a guy like that put one over on her.

Chapter
THREE

alley didn't like being in a guy's place, least of all, Roady Dean's. Not that she'd been in guys' rooms much. She hadn't. Just Roady's, to pick up Didi.

She stood in the hall in front of his door. The floor, the walls, seemed to be throbbing. Didi would have unlocked the door a few minutes ago. Sometimes, Roady left the door unlocked all evening so dudes could come visit anytime, but not when Didi was with him.

Talley braced herself, took a deep breath. Roady's not a boy like the guys in school. I mean, I can't tell what he is, she thought. Maybe he's a *man*. But his dad's a *man*. Poppy's a *man*. Roady is . . . something else.

She turned the knob and walked in. Discord screamed and crashed into her, like a furious, rushing attack of heavy rhythms. Crash Metal music, so loud, Talley bent double trying to get away from it. "Turn it down!" she shouted at the forms under the covers across the room.

Talley clamped her hands over her ears and threw herself into the nearest chair. Huddled against the table there, she squeezed her eyes shut to escape the scream-

25

ing guitars, the howling voice. Her breath came shallowly. "Oh, God, turn it down!" But who could hear her above the noise? A minute later, her pulse hammered in her temples and she knew she was going to be sick.

Noise ceased, suddenly. She felt like someone had knocked the wind out of her. The silence was intense, filling the room. It settled down in her chest like a cool breeze. "Oh, wow!" she murmured, breathing deeply to calm herself. Sometimes, the music affected her like this. Sickening. Other times, she just got a headache.

She kept her eyes closed a moment longer, then opened them on the stark, somber room.

Roady's guy's place was where he did everything that other guys did in their homes, or at other people's houses, because Roady didn't have a home any longer. His place was his home. His dad set him up in it, paid for it, paid for Roady's food. He actually gave Roady too much money, which Roady spent on "peculiar substances," was what Didi called what he spent his money on, and electronic equipment. And Didi. Roady was into all kinds of preamps and tuners and absolute power. Into heaviest metal, what he called the groove. Stones because they were way bad and Dead and Zeppelin, even Kiss out of nostalgia. Talley couldn't tell the groove, like Quiet Riot, from punk and new wave and didn't care to. She only knew it was loud. It didn't sound like nothing. And Roady's headbanger head was nothing. Empty.

Didi gathered her clothes from a straight chair by the bed. Stood there in her bra and panties looking at Talley. "Hi, babe," she said, her voice husky from having to scream at Roady so he could hear her above his noise. "I'm sorry. Forgot to turn it down." Talking about the music. "Don't *even* hear it anymore."

"Girl . . ." Talley said, feeling uncomfortable. They

were used to seeing one another's bodies. They were runners and runners knew their bodies at rest and in motion, as few did who were not athletes. Never was Talley embarrassed by Didi's or her own nudity when they were in the locker room. But it really upset her to have Didi walk around in just her underwear with Roady Dean in the room, probably naked under the covers.

Talley felt her face go hot. She turned away.

"I'm going," Didi said. "Why you have to make . . ."

"I didn't say nothing," Talley said, softly.

She glanced at Roady lying on his back in bed, his arm flung over his closed eyes. "Hi, Roady," she said, as Didi closed the bathroom door to get dressed.

Roady grunted. Moved his legs under the sheet, slid his head around under his arm. Blinked at her a long moment. "Who's that?" he said.

"It's me," she said. He usually recognized her right away. "Came to pick up Didi."

"Ohhh," he said. "What day . . . is it . . . Friday?"

"No, it's Tuesday," she said.

"And I'm . . ."

"You're Roady Dean." Days like this, he was the last straw between her and her tears.

"Roady . . ."

"Roady Dean Lewis," she said. "Your girl is Didi Lillian Adair. She hates her middle name and she's in love with you."

Roady often woke up after even a short sleep not knowing who he was or what day it was. No matter that she told him who Didi was. Quite often, he didn't know Didi the first time he saw her after waking. Once, he'd awakened from a far-out dream thinking Didi was a replicate from science fiction. He'd thrown her out of the house, almost threw her down the fire stairs. With Talley hanging on his back, shouting for help, trying to shake him out of it.

"Roady?"

"Yeah?"

"You know me?" she asked.

"Talley," he said.

"Yeah. Now, you cool! You know who Roady is—and who Didi is?" She no longer asked how much stuff he'd had. It didn't do any good to know. It just made her sick to care about somebody who took all kinds of stuff for days. Her Poppy would disown her if he knew she hung out with people like that.

"Who . . . ?"

She sighed. "You and Didi who I named you," she said, lightly, feeling as blue as she could feel. Hate this place! All that shiny equipment he have—tape decks and speakers and discs and all. Thousands and thousands a dollars. And for music so loud you can't even understand a word the singer sing? "You and Didi A White Romance, remember?" But Didi always hated the name she'd given them.

"Ohhhh . . . Oh, yeah! Me and Didi. Great—ha-a-a-a! That's right, that's a trip. I remember now," Roady said.

He stretched out, let the sheet slip to his waist. Had his hands behind his head. Closed his eyes again. He grinned. Talley knew he was remembering. She had to smile, herself.

A White Romance. The beginning of school when it happened. September. All these new students all over, in every class. Couldn't walk down her old halls without seeing strangers.

All those be-white kids for the first time. Talley nodded to herself. Sounds silly now, but then, it was *strange*. White kids with pink, pimply faces and white hands and white necks, all over the place. They *smelled* different. Couldn't tell not one hand from another, nor not one face. And *blonds.* Real blond girls who looked blue they were so white. All us trying not to be uncool, not looking at them too hard for a while. And they doing the same.

A couple a days go by and it's cool, nothing's not so bad and nothing bad seems to be going down. Kids start scoping, kind of. Sign up for sports and gym together and all. Big sports he-roes and her-roes, chill out! It's all right, be friendly in the gym or on the track. Everybody going out their way not to start nothing. Some be-white girls nice to everyone. But kind of standoffish.

Talley was like that, too. Always did hang loose by herself. Everybody knew her. She talked to everyone, but she had no tight friendships. Poppy said that was the best way. *"Don't get into the 'clicks,' Talley, they trouble."*

But you know, the be-whites have more clicks than anybody. Even the guys. And that was what started it. They acting so snooty. But they's always some be-black hotheads and be-white "aggressives" with an attitude, have to get into it.

Swiftly, Talley laid it all out in her mind again. What hit you first was the noise and the sweat. By Friday, kids were bold. Three thousand teenagers going out of their minds from being po-*lite*, ready to break out for the weekend. There were incidents of their shouting and cussing at one another in the halls. One home and one be-white dude standing in the hall, staring at each other for five minutes. Each one had a hand on the other's arm. They stood like statues. Silent, staring each other down, surrounded by students.

Until a teacher separated them evenly. She didn't grab one or the other; she touched them at the same time and flung their hands away.

"Get to your classes, both of you. Get out of the corridor!"

After that, half of the student body was terrified something might happen to them, someone might get hurt.

Little freshmen looking like they're going to cry-baby, buh-cause they're afraid the whole place is going to puh-loom, Jim, Talley remembered. Poof! Nothing left but the smoke. Be-black and be-white never been in so close to each other in their lives. Can't tell which side is most afraid. Scared their pictures get in the paper for breaking the rules. Then, the moms and dads kick them on they *sasses*. The shame of their school being called a bad place.

Nobody knew why, but everybody felt it. Coming down. Real trouble, not AWR but trouble.

Somebody set it off. Suddenly, it had started.

Didi came out of the bathroom, dressed now, ready to split from Roady's place. But she still had her makeup to put on. She had to blow out her hair. She'd taken a shower. Girl took forever.

"I won't be long," Didi murmured. She went over to the bed, sat down to put her socks and shoes on. Roady wrapped his arm around her waist. Curled up around her back, looking like a little kid. Big, gangly Roady.

"I know who you arr-ruh," he said, like a little kid.

"Who-oo am I?" Didi sang back to him.

Talley, watching, pushed A White Romance back as far away as she could.

I was minding my own business that Friday, when the trouble started, she recalled. There must have been three hundred kids in the hallway. Their Magnet corridors looked like long side streets—no parking!—school was so huge. It felt like all of the three hundred were coming at Talley. Suddenly she had felt trapped.

"Victor, help me!" she called. Holding her books in front of her, pressed flat against a locker. The lock dug painfully into her lower back. "Help me!"

It was as if Victor Davis was a projectile of some kind, propelled down the corridor. He was shoving and knocking students out of his way as he went.

Handsome, she had thought, fleetingly, one of those muscled-and-lean sports guys out of reach. He'd grown up in The Neighborhood just as Talley had. He wasn't quite running. Something about the crowd suddenly scared her witless. Two uglies, tallest, two hip guys in the middle of the pack. Instantly, Talley singled them out. She recognized maybe ten or so kids besides Victor. Surrounded, she felt faint, like she would melt into the floor. She was on the small side.

Victor was the finest athlete in the used-to-be-black school. And now, probably one of the best in the Magnet, if not the baddest. He was on the Student Council. He patrolled the halls this year with his be-white counterpart, Stuart, who was equally well-known to the be-white kids. Victor was a great soccer sweeper, a great ball handler. He was so tough, he never had to get in a fight. He could fight using just his feet. Nobody wanted to take him on. Victor had always been nice to Talley. She'd known him all her life. She respected him.

"Victor, help!"

"Talley, stay where you are!" he called to her, as kids swept by, slamming their fists into lockers to show they weren't afraid. Noise of lockers clanged endlessly.

"Victor! What's happening?" Get me out! was what Talley felt like saying. But she didn't want him to see how scared she was. Terror welled up in her without warning.

He stood in front of her a moment, making a sandwich

31

of her between him and the locker. He shielded her completely.

"Don't move, no matter what," he said, "'cause, carry."

Because it was the blades you worried about. Everybody "carry." Talley had a stiletto in her purse for self-defense. Be-white students coming to the Magnet "carried" as well. No one kept a carry in a locker because of the periodic sweeps Security made. Yet some had scores to settle. Couldn't find the one they wanted, the one who looked at them wrong, or said something to them wrong, they might "carry" it out and cut on who was handy.

Victor and Stuart reached out, grabbed the two biggest uglies, be-black and be-white. "Both be bad," Talley would say, later. That's why the kids were panicking out of the way. The two dudes were lifted off their feet, almost held like rag-boys. Talley couldn't see their faces. Victor slammed one down, bent him double, as Stuart handled the other one. The two bad dudes struggled but they couldn't get loose. Then, the hall-noise and movement came to a halt.

"Uh-huh!" Victor said. "Everybody stay right where it is. You move, and you break rule number eleven. We're not going to have some scene here, you dig?"

"What it is? What'd they do?"

"Don't you talk when I'm talking!" Victor yelled down the hall: "I said, this stuff is not coming down. Nothing going to happen, so keep still.

"Now. You ugly clowns get up and ac' like you got some sense!" Spoken to the uglies bent over. Victor and Stuart let them loose. Jerked them to their feet and shoved them forward. "Now, hand over!"

"I got nuth-thin," the be-black said, keeping his hand inside his unbuttoned shirt.

The be-white spread his hands toward Stuart, to say

32

he had nothing. His face was beet red. He would have taken a chance, maybe swing on Stuart to get away. But he saw how both Stuart and Victor towered over everybody, both bigger than he was, even, by at least an inch, and changed his mind.

"We're giving you a chance," Victor told them. "If you want us to call Security, we will. We know you carry. Hand over and don't bring it in here again."

"Do I get it back?" be-black ask him. Talley had seen the guy but didn't know him. One of the outsiders; not from The Neighborhood. Wouldn't know him if you paid her.

"You get the back of my fist, brutha. Hand over and that's it," Victor said.

"I ain't handing nuth-thin in front of the whole schoo'," the be-black said through clenched teeth.

"You do what I *tell* you, man," Victor said. "You hand over the carry." Then, he said, loud, to all standing around, "Move! Everybody. Move on out!" He turned his head to the side, and said so softly, "You too, Talley." She was still against the locker where he had first shielded her.

Talley walked quickly away and everybody else did the same. She never did see the hand-over. Guessed nobody else did, either, except Victor and Stuart, and the two uglies.

The Student Council black and white teams put a lid down on every hallway. They fanned out everywhere— lunchroom, gyms, playing fields, rest rooms.

Word was that kids had stampeded when they heard someone yell, "Fight!" But that rumor was false, was stopped in two minutes flat. There were Council teams to cool everybody. Say the teams had been set up eight months before school opened. Say they had drills and rehearsals about calming crowds and disarming students. That rumor got started and the Council teams let it run around.

Talley was shaking for the rest of the day. You could feel the tension, but it had evaporated mostly by lunch. Seemed most kids didn't want any mess. Not the bloods or the pales. There had been some of both on the outside the first week until they could be-*have*.

Mr. Bagley, the principal, had kicked dumb-*basses* quickly, and fair enough to satisfy most. The AP, who was from The Neighborhood, read off the list of "anybodys," the students called it, as though it were a group of viruses. They put it into their own kind of rapping: *"Anybody caught in the halls without a pass, honey, anybody smoking in the johns or using drugs in the johns— ooh! or anywhere else or keeping stash in their lockers. Anybody outside when they 'spose' to be inside, anybody 'using language,' anybody 'signifying,' anybody threatening, anybody kissing on the stairs—mercy!—or worse in the locker rooms, anybody wrestling in the halls, skateboarding in the halls, smacking, tripping, kneeing, punching, breaking in or out, or break-dancing—gets his/her-sass kicked—oh, yeah!"* Couldn't do nothing, Jim.

"Todd Lamont, Joshua Fred Douglass, don't you come near this place, you hear?" Mr. Judd, the AP, told them that first incident. "Until both of you can act like *gentlemen.*"

"My dad's gonna have to come see you," Todd Lamont threatened. A big football dude. "I can't afford no mark against me. Me, gettin' a scholarship."

"Son, you tell Dooley Lamont I'll meet him on the squash court tomorrow, regular time," the AP said.

Talley had laughed when she heard that! They say

Todd Lamont had looked so stunned. Didn't know the be-black AP had been smashing rackets with his be-white daddy. Probably playing sports together was part of the plan to get the new parents familiar with the staff of the school.

Fred Douglass guffawed and got Mr. Judd on his case. "When you do get back in school, you've got a week's detention, Fred."

"Aw, Mr. Judd, man, I ain't done sh—"

"Don't say it, Fred, or you're out for a month."

"Mr. Judd, man? Shoot! Y'all ac' like we criminals, suh-um," Fred had whined.

"Yeah, what are we, criminals?" Todd Lamont said. The two finally went off together, looking back kind of sad over their shoulders at the AP.

Love it! Talley thought. She had heard the same basic story in two separate classes. Word always got around about everybody doing wrong. But she still couldn't figure out why she had panicked so in the first instance in the hallway. A suffocating sensation had come over her.

Like I was going to choke to death right there, she thought now.

Then, AWR happened. It happened at the very end of the second week of the fall semester. She'd been heading down the hall to her locker. Wide, carpeted hall, when AWR showed up.

A blooming silk flower, anytime, any season, she thought now.

The Magnet, the Colonel Glenn, was a cool school with carpets all up and down the halls and sideways in every room. The suburban students were amazed at their carpets. "You guys just install this," someone asked, "because of us coming?"

"*What?* In-stall what?" a home said, although he knew

35

some of the carpeting was brand new. "Buddy, car-pet was *born* on these floors, shi . . . you Nawth Americans are *privileged* to walk on 'em." Said in such a way that it was funny.

Now there were only the few students, the minority, who still wanted to start up something else.

Chapter
FOUR

X-sightment! Somebody write *X-sightment!* everywhere on bathroom stall doors and on the blackboards, too.

Then kids start in graffitiing the student body down: *"Whitey skin de-seased, mutant." "Black scum trash Africa."* When it started on the walls of classrooms, there were more detentions and several assemblies about mutual respect. Assemblies came down usually first period. That gave the entire student body the chance to kick way back and get some rest. But the graffiti never stopped.

The grown-folks, the so-called adults had to get their two cents into it. Talley lived on a nice tree-lined street, right off a main avenue, where there were mostly small but neat houses. She and her father lived in a two-story apartment building that had been built to blend in with the rest of The Neighborhood, the good parts. Everybody in their building was nice. Everybody on her street worked hard. There were no shiftless cheats on their block, her Poppy swore to her there weren't.

"We'll keep them out of this apartment house," he'd

told her more than once. And he'd told her, "Talley, you're a Barbour, watch who you hang with. Your school changed now with the consolidation. You be careful. Can't tell what kind comin' from othertown. Don't bring nothing with light eyes into this house."

Can you believe that? she mused.

The first time her Poppy had seen her running with Didi, he'd stopped dead in his tracks, watched them flash by. They were running down the street with a whole pack of girls who thought they could distance-run. They had been divided from the rest of the gym class. With an instructor leading and a department aide following, they were to run two miles into the side streets and come on back and finish up on the school track. That's what the Parent/Teacher Association called "reclaiming the community." Let everybody see that *all* kids belong running through. Get used to seeing them. Exhausted, unable to make the miles, sometimes. Sitting on the curbs, resting on corners. Let the town around the school see kids all colors together, working, running, learning and getting strong together. The high-school students were the community; the community should look out for all of them.

It was true. It could work, was working half the time. Only, it got upsetting sometimes when there were large school events. The ladies and men from othertown, the suburbs, came riding up in real pretty cars. Most folks in the heart of town didn't have that kind of first-class equipment. Talley's dad had a VW, which wasn't new, but it ran most of the time. Didi's mother had a Buick Riviera, which she hated but had got in the divorce settlement. It was stolen once; she had been quick, she'd been home and they caught the stealers before they could strip it and cut it up.

Buick Riviera the favorite car of thieves. Talley didn't know why. But folks from othertown had fine equipment, like BMWs and sporty things Talley didn't know the names of. There were true rich kids in the Colonel Glenn now, although Talley hadn't found them out yet. She supposed most of them were the blond girls.

But you couldn't call Didi and her mom othertown. They didn't live in The Neighborhood, either. They lived on the fringe, farther out than Roady, on the far side of industries, between the industries and the othertown. Little row apartment houses, scrunged up, no trees to speak of. Long, long streets on the fringes of the city, where city streetcar lines ended. Edge of nowhere.

But the first time I see Didi, I think she's othertown, Talley was thinking. How'm I suppose to know some be-white live on out there, city-fringe? So a magnet draws Didi, too. So all be-white won't be-rich, either, and a lot of them aren't so bad, either. Lesson number one.

But that day, we are running through The Neighborhood around the Magnet. And we had to go bump into Poppy. Talley had no doubt other grown-ups of The Neighborhood felt just the way he did.

"He liked to wear me out, talking down everything," she told Didi the next day. "Poppy scolding me for an hour when I get home from school, all about mixing with be-white girls."

"What's he think a magnet's all about? What was he doing out there, off from work," Didi asked, "spying on you?"

"Sure, you know he was," Talley said. "Pretending he's forgot something at home. He want to see if I sneak in there, something."

"Well, he got what he didn't expect," Didi had said.

"Just because there's some be-white, he upset," Talley

39

said. "They want the Magnet in The Neighborhood but they don't want all us kids mixing together. Tell you, it's the grown folks is the trouble."

Leave us alone, we be fine, she thought now, up in Roady's place. Didi and me are close. I mean, I trusted her from the first. We hang together. I mean, when she's not hanging with Roady Dean over there. But that's something else. I ain't into that, yet.

Deep inside, Talley felt a gnawing. She watched Roady stretch himself long in the tangled sheets. Sheet rode down so low on his hips, his white, sick-looking body, that she had to turn away and not look again. She watched Didi blow her hair in front of the hall mirror. After a minute, she no longer had to watch her friend. For the little mouse was gnawing to get in her hope chest. If she could only shut down her mind for an hour! But she couldn't. It was always going, showing off and telling on her. She, the little mouse, suspected there were treasures to keep tight, to hold on to. Homes called her treasures "goodies." That's how she knew they were there and worth something. At least to the homes.

"Hey, Roxanne, babie-two-shoes, put your goodies in my palms awhile."

No time for you, home, too.

Calling her Roxanne from that rap song they called baaad and whack. Old song, now, about three homeboys trying to get it on with this awesome chick, too. Calling somebody Roxanne was inner sit-tay to describe a "young lady" like Talley, herself, who refused to give them the time of day. *"You think you's cute, Roxanne,"* they called down the halls, *"I know where you lives, where you comes from and what you old man got. He got nuth-thin, so come offen the highwire, Roxanne."*

Don't waste my time talking to just any kind, she

thought. Mostly I talk to the track and soccer field, like Victor. They nice. They understand about how you must take care of yourself inside and out your body, Talley thought. But if you don't talk to the others once in a while, they will put a name on you. Worse than Roxanne. Like you one-of-them-things—girls they lay down with. And in The Neighborhood, you-get-a-name, you have it for your life, too. Don't eveh talk-in-close to no be-white boys, either.

But I have, Talley thought. I mean I did, just now. Well not really talk-in-close talking. But he already call me Roxanne, too, but it won't be a bad name. I talk to that . . . that long-hair, brown-hair boy in this building.

Curiosity rose in her about the long-haired guy. It came swiftly.

He look at me, just like the homes do, too. Only, his is light eyes.

It, the curiosity, fell away just as swiftly. Light eyes were always dangerous, whether they belonged to be-white or half and half, the mixed.

I break the first rule. Don't even think about breaking some of those kind of rules.

Poppy. *"Don't disappoint me, young lady."* Poppy, talking inside her. *"And here, carry this."* He had given her her carry. The real-ivory-handled stiletto. Slender, tapering blade. He had bought the dagger especially for her. Not any kind of cheap item, either. Not any of the home babies had anything nearly like it.

"But, Poppy, it might hurt somebody."

"Young lady, don't be dumb. Somebody try to hurt you, you got to be prepared to hurt him hard, first. It might be your only chance. Hit first and hit to hurt. And don't stick around to find out how bad the wounded be doing."

"Or even if I've made a mistake? Striking out first? Maybe he, someone, actually mean me no harm, Poppy."

"Young lady, they always after the defenseless and trusting, like you. If you make a mistake, it's self-defense. Let him prove otherwise. You got to protect yourself. Time this neighborhood get through with him, he going to wish he run into some other young lady, some other where, and not you."

Too much always going on inside her. Where was inside! Talley didn't know. Sometimes, it didn't seem to be in her head. Some kind of longing she had seemed to be on the landscape or on the windows of buildings, on the street signs, anywhere she looked. She guessed it was pressed there wherever she looked so it could touch her heart and make her so sad whenever it felt like it.

Poppy. Man, I don't know. I wouldn't dare do what Didi's up to, else Poppy kill me. And it's not wrong, like he think it something dirty. Didi's about the nicest person and she's not bad, she's not a sinner because she loves somebody.

Didi's my friend. You stick by your friends. She stick by me come high water or what. So how was I to know there would come AWR? Hadn't come across a dude like Roady yet.

It been the fall and no track until spring, shoot. But I run, always. Then, I see this note posted on the information board. "Who wants to run? Didi Adair."

"That be-white girl in my typing class?" I say to myself. So next time in class, I say, "You Didi Adair? What you mean, who wants to run? You Didi Adair, want to run? That what it mean?"

I'm tough, see, start out. You don't know how they're going to act, once you pin them down to something. You

42

never know, she could've written the note and never thought any be-black going to come up to her about it. I mean, some of them looking in your face like you're not there at all. Smile, like they just remember you are human, but they don't want to be reminded every day. There's some kind like that at Colonel Glenn. Not all of them, but a few. They don't bother me. I say what Poppy says: Don't evah try to stop me doing what I'm doing, Mazie Jane.

Didi looking at me a real long time before she answered, Talley remembered. "I'm not into no soccer team anymore," she'd said, "but I like running."

It was then that Talley realized she was looking in the face of a beautiful girl.

I mean, blond and beautiful, Talley was thinking. I thought she just had to be rich, too.

You could talk about the stereotype be-white American girl anytime you wanted to. But Didi Adair was amazing the way she looked.

Looking like Daryl Hannah, some terrific actress. No attitude. I thought so the first I saw Didi and I still think so. She's not some blank blond girl.

Could've been a movie star, Didi looking that good. Furthermore, she looking at you up-front, like you there with her, she want you there. She just looked at you like you are close in with her; she cares to have you there. Her voice just straight at you—not sweet, not phony, not high-school, or cheerleader, or tough. It is Didi. It is real. Her eyes real gray-blue. And she is always nice to everybody. But she loves this boy and she cannot help herself.

We'd barely talk. We'd run, though, Jim. It's like, you get to know somebody when you run with them all the time. And she the only girl besides me in high school that can stand to run in the ice cold. Cold days come more. But I didn't know that then. I just knew we were running through the fall. Running miles and miles. Man it was *intense* running! Da-ag! Check it out! Ohhh! Leaves falling still! I love to run with somebody pacing beside me and the leaves are chasing us both.

And then, she just start in talking to me some. We had the leaves scrunching under our running shoes. Long stretches, we didn't say a word. But that was all right.

It was quick how me and Didi and Roady hit it off. Well, Didi and me, anyway. I mean, I never ever have a friend be-white before. I asked her, did she ever have a color-friend, be-black? And she said, she couldn't because there wasn't a one anywhere she went to school out there. Now, you know, I never thought about them be segregated, it so sad, too. Not like all us, together. They don't seem to be in close like The Neighborhood. You forget how big a city this is and how many schools still are not a magnet.

But about Roady. Who can tell where Roady is and he's looking straight in your face? Roady some other else. Everybody be-black or be-white loves that child. I know, some grown-ups would say he is bad news. But he's really not, only to himself, maybe. It's like, he brings all us in to feeling how, there-but-for-the-grace-of-God-go—any one of us, Jim. Everybody takes care of him. It's not like he's able to do anything. It's like he's . . . dis-*abled*. Like, someone who's lost part of himself, no fault of his own. Keeps on going all by himself, though. You can't stop him, you want to help him. He's dis-*turbed*! But he's got some special sweetness and you don't got it but you want to get as close to it as you can.

I remember, all the kids start one day doing d-i-s, dis, about Roady. And that's when you understand Roady's

going to be the one that all-us forget is different from us.
"Roady dis-*spelled*," someone say.

"Roady dis-*armed*."

"Dis-*graced*."

"*Dis-jointed*."

"Roady dis-*owned*, dis-*allowed* and *dis-appeared!*"

"Roady *dis-grun-toled*, Jim."

He'd give you the clothes off his back and I've seen
him do it for somebody. He won't see color or have or
haven't. He's got it all, but he won't care. Maybe that's
why everybody think he so funny in school, and everybody's friend. They don't got it; and if they had it, they
sure wouldn't give it up. So he's not like anybody else.
He's *somethin-else.*

"Funny peculiar, or funny ha-ha?" Talley asked herself
under her breath. Didi's mama always did say that to
her.

"That girl is so funny all the time," Talley might tell
Mrs. Vera Adair. Mrs. Adair would look at her over her
tiny rectangles of glasses she had. She'd hold her paper
in one hand and she would say, "Funny peculiar, or
funny ha-ha?"

Talley would think how Roady was something else
and say, "Funny peculiar."

But she and Didi and Mrs. Adair would have
their heads close together. It was like, well, Talley
thought, it was like loving sisters and the mama at that
table in the dining room of the Adair two-person apartment.

Talley thought about how the man-of-the-house had
split some time ago. She knew that in her own house, it
had been her Poppy forced her mama to leave.

I mean, I have to live with him, Talley thought. But her

Poppy expected a woman to wait on him all the time. Don't wear makeup, or short skirts. Don't go out with your woman friends. Be there when he gets there. Don't have any opinions of your own, not in front of him. He knows it all. No sane wife could live with that, would want to live with a man like her Poppy for long.

Chapter
FIVE

alley grinned at Didi's profile. Girl was finished drying and combing out her baby-fine blow-hair.
Not too much time had passed. There was a glint in
Talley's eyes not unlike the glow of Didi's long locks in
the light. Talley had been thinking and remembering a
mile a minute.

"You recall A White Romance?" she asked her friend.

Didi shivered. Looked away. "Talley, come on, we have
to go," she said.

Roady Dean laughed, lying there across the room. Pale
fish body, relaxed, naked, more than half out of the
sheets.

"Roady Dean, cover your private self," Talley said.
Dared not look.

"Don't look, then," Roady murmured, hooting. "A
White Romance" he sang off-key, to the tune of "A Fine
Romance" from some old movie. Talley thought she'd
seen that old movie on cable. Anyway, she recognized
the song.

Roady Dean had told her that because of cable, anybody could learn the history of music. "Roady, I couldn't care less," she had told him.

"Sad sorrow," he'd said, when halfway coherent. "I can't rock steady. Cannot metal-groove. To raise the arms of thousands; make the love sign—the horns of Satan—with my own band! My own videos! And have twenty, fifty thousands scream and freak. Maaaan! What a trip . . . but I can't play nothin'."

"No, but you don't have to," Talley said, "'cause you A White Romance." Sounding as if she were playing with him, but she wasn't. She meant AWR in his favor.

"Me, A White Romance?" he said, lightly.

"Yeah, you know you are," she said.

"Tell me about it," he said, grinning.

"That's enough!" Didi said, snapping her makeup case shut. "Let's get out of here."

"Didi . . ." Talley began.

"I told you not to call us that," Didi said.

"Didi, nobody thinks anything . . ."

"Yes, they do!" Didi yelled. "I hate being called that behind my back. Buh-cause it's a real put-down."

"No it's not!" Talley said.

"I'm sorry it ever happened!" Didi mumbled, looking ready to cry.

"Why you have to smear that stuff on?" Roady called across to Didi. Changing the subject. He was talking about the makeup she wore—a little more than was necessary. Talley could see Roady's red-coated eyes from where she stood across the room.

"Roady, you look like a stupid werewolf," Didi said.

"How?" Roady said, slurring the words. "Does Roady wear a wolf? Road, de-wear. Ha-a-a-a! That's funny. Road, de-wear, Read de-wear, Ready-wear!"

"Oooh, he's so simple!" Talley bent over, laughing.

"Be quiet," Didi said, "he's not *that* funny." But she was grinning. She shook her head, giggling. Roady was so pitiful. Sometimes, by the end of the day when Talley and Didi were too tired of keeping him straight on, of themselves, even, they broke up laughing at him.

Roady rose out of bed. The sheets slid to his knees. He stamped his feet, trying to get free, standing up then sinking in the mattress. Sheets rode his ankles, tightening. Suddenly, he was off-balance. His arms flailed. He commenced toppling. Blue-white body with thin arms and legs, slanting, naked. He came wheeling out of bed. He sprawled, smacking against bare floors. And spilled sickeningly, the color of soap-dirty dishwater.

Talley screamed. She covered her face with her hands so as not to see all he had. A boy, whatever Roady was, a guy, all open like that.

"Oh, Roady! God!" Didi, rushing to him.

"Oooh," Talley moaned, realizing he might've hurt himself. She felt ashamed. I'm so mean! she thought.

"Talley, help me with him!" Panicked, Didi yelled at her.

"Tell him to cover up himself," Talley muttered. She felt scared of him.

"You stupid . . . You're disgusting, not him!" Didi said through clamped teeth. She grabbed a sheet and threw it over his hips. Talley came over, not looking, staring at the floor.

"Help me get him up," Didi said, in an even tone. She was back in control. "Roady, you have to help us."

"Here," she said to Talley, "grab him from the back. You think you can do that without being insulted by the sight?"

"But he's . . . he's a guy," she managed. Nude! she

thought. She didn't want to touch his white skin. Oooh, man, what would Poppy say?

"I swearda-god!" Didi shouted. Made Talley wince. "I suppose you never seen a guy with no clothes on before."

There was silence as they exerted themselves getting Roady back on the bed.

Didi gave Talley a swift, startled glance. "Not even your own pop?" she said. "Oh, I forgot. No, 'course not, coming from where you come from."

"What's that suppose to mean?" Talley shot back. Her anger flashed like heat lightning, cold and hot at once.

"You *would* take it wrong," Didi said, and turned to Roady Dean. "Honey? You all right? Where did you think you were going?"

Roady lay perfectly still, his eyes on the ceiling. "I was going to do . . . something. I was going to dance . . . A White Romance."

"Sure you were," Didi said, softly. She might hate the term, A White Romance, but Roady Dean thought it made him macho. "Roady, you sure you all right? I haveta go in a minute."

"You leaving?" he said, languidly. "I'm not hurt."

"Mommy's got supper," Didi said. She hugged him tightly, her face against the side of his face.

Talley slid her foot along the floor.

"Did we have fun?" Roady asked Didi, holding on to her. They were cheek to cheek.

"We had a real good time, baby boy," she murmured, dreamily.

Roady moved his mouth but no words came. When Didi realized he was silent-talking, she turned his face to her and read his lips.

"I'm not getting what you're saying," she told him. "Roady? Speak words, hon."

He looked at her, uncomprehending. Then, his voice just seemed to come of itself. "Put my metal on."

"Which one do you want on?" she asked him.

"Put Priest on," he said, his tone detached.

Talley knew that was the rock group, Judas Priest. She'd heard enough of metal to know who she liked better than whom she didn't. She could now distinguish some Priest songs from Quiet Riot's *Metal Health* debut album, as long as Roady turned the volume down to about medium ear damage. She sighed. She would be forever on the outside of loving metal music. She did like Judas Priest better than most metal groups. But she was partial to the black sound. She liked Kool and the Gang, Tina, and Stevie, better than anything. The Pointers were cool, and Whitney Houston and Lionel Richie, too. They all could groove, sometimes.

Talley loved the way young black singers were almost all tall and skinny. And all shades of brown. Roady just laughed at her when she said stuff like that. But it was nice she could say stuff like that to him and Didi. Finally, he would go into a crazy fit of laughter and cough himself into gagging.

Didi up-volume on Priest so high, that Talley felt her hair was on end. Didi made sure Roady Dean was all right. Kissing him all over his face and hair. Hugging him close as she could. And then: "I'm outta here!" she hollered into the metal blast. And blew her boy a kiss.

They left Roady where he lay. Didi locked the door behind them. Silent, going down in the elevator. Outside, everything seemed now fresh and healthy, after rain.

"Can't see how you can leave him like that," Talley

said. "Does he know to eat some food? One minute, you all over him like white on rice. Next minute, you leave him all alone."

"Oh? Now you care that I leave him? You can't stand to look at him," Didi said.

"I can stand it, too. I can too stand it. I did stand it. I helped you."

"Yeah, after I made you."

"Well, I don't know about guys so much," Talley said. "I don't know how it is. I mean . . . you and me, we're in different places when it comes to guys."

"Tell me about it!" Didi said. All at once, she flowed into her pace as if her stride form had been there waiting in the street for her. She entered into it with grace. No effort at all. Talley did the same.

They were running. The rain started again; it rained lightly on them. Didi's hair shone with the rain in the light of streetlamps. Talley looked at it. Didi looked at Talley's hair, grinned, nodded at her.

"Mine do the same?" Talley murmured. "All glinty?"

" 'Course!" Didi said. Their hair, glistening with rain droplets. It was like the rain held the night coming on.

"Feels so good," Talley said. I don't want to look like her, she thought. I don't want that straw hair that won't curl. Didi get in the sun, she turns red all a sudden, like somebody said something to make her jump back.

Be cool about her and me. Chill it on out. Friends, that's it. I don't want to be just like her.

"We got a paper to write for English," Talley thought to say. "You going to do it?"

"Might," Didi said. "But not tonight. I better call Roady tonight."

"Shoot, Didi, you'll talk an hour!"

"Well, you and Mama always talking a mile a minute!" Didi laughed.

"Very funny, but you better had start to study. Don't be too sure your grades can make college the way they be."

"I'm going to marry Roady. Get a job," Didi said. A thin line of perspiration clung to her upper lip.

"When are you going to marry him! Before you graduate? You all getting married before you graduate!"

"If I get pregnant, I will," Didi said.

"Oh, my Lord!" Talley sighed, broke stride, started again. "You better not get pregnant! Don't you . . . don't you . . . use . . ."

"I swearda—Talley! No, we don't! So what? I don't care."

"That is *so* stupid!" Talley cried, smacking her head from the shock.

"What do you know about it?" Didi said. She punched Talley lightly on the arm. "Dummy! I use the pill. Anyway, I wouldn't mind having a little baby. I'd call her Roadene, you know? After Roady, and Didi, me. Roadene. She'd be all ours, our little girl."

"Like a toy," Talley said. "You been thinkin' about it—having a toy! You just like all the rest, think babies are some *dolls*."

"All the rest, what?" Didi said, looking at her. "All the rest who get pregnant or the rest who are bad because they do it with somebody?" She didn't miss a stride. She laughed, tossing her blow-hair.

Talley shook her head, as if to clear it. She didn't like hearing about pregnancy. Every time she saw a girl her age with her belly sticking out, she wanted to hide her face.

"Poppy says girls think babies be toys until the little

dolls first pee on their party dresses. Then, they think twice and it's too late."

"He would say that," Didi said.

"It's not true?"

"I don't got a party dress," Didi said. "I party with Roady. We are our own party of two."

Well, maybe so, Talley thought. A White Romance. She wasn't in love like Didi. What Didi did with Roady she wouldn't dare do. Sex.

"I'm too shy," she said. Before she knew it, they were talking about it. Always, before she knew it, she was trying to find out.

"Look, when you're ready, it'll happen," Didi told her.

"No, it won't!" Talley said. "I don't even know a guy I could even want to kiss." Her insides felt empty, cleaned out.

"Sure you do," Didi said. "You just scared to think about it. You so scared of your daddy! But I bet if you kicked back and thought about it on a Saturday when there's no school and time to rest and think about private things. You know, just don't jump outta bed the first thing, 'cause Poppy's going to holler if you don't start in cleaning up the place."

"He never hollers at me."

"Okay, he won't love you as much if you stop being his slave."

"Shut up, Didi, you don't know."

"Okay, I'm sorry. But it makes me mad. How come you suppose to be his housekeeper?"

"He works, he takes care of me, too," Talley said.

Didi didn't say anything. They were nearly to the bus stop. Talley wanted to ask what she would ask at least once a week. She tried to say it in a new way somewhat each time. But she had to ask. She had to know.

"Is it . . . is it always the same . . . when you and Roady . . . you know!"

Didi grinned. "Girl! Noooo!"

"Then, how's it different?" Talley asked.

" 'Cause we're different," Didi said. "Depends. It can be sooo much!"

"Yeah? How?"

She told Talley all that she could bring herself to put into words. Didi never did keep it in her head the way Talley did. "It hurts, at first."

Talley felt her insides seem to fill with cold. "It does?" she murmured.

"Yeah, I told you that. If the guy is . . . I love Roady, though. It won't always be pretty, like the movies, I mean, the real thing, when you do it. I mean, it is, but it's so *real*. Makes me cry, girls like you think I'm bad. I don't mean you, don't look at me like that! But then, crying about it makes me *mad*. Roady will hold me as long as I want when I get all uptight about it. 'Screw the hateful,' he says."

Talley held her breath. She couldn't say what she was looking for. But what it was seemed to fall away from what Didi could tell her. She never could find out quite what she wanted to know. Like, but what do you mean, "if the guy is . . ."—what? She wanted to ask, "If the guy is *rough? Big?* What?" But she was too shy to ask, too ready to be shamed by her ignorance. She knew but she didn't *quite* know. She needed to get down to the nitty-gritty of it. But in her heart, she'd much rather just know the romance of it.

"Is it wonderful, though?" she finally thought to say. That was better.

"It's probably different for everybody," Didi said. "Probably pretty special, though. And wonderful." She'd said so before.

"Sounds so funny to me," Talley said.

"Why?"

"Because it should be the same for everybody. I mean how can it be wonderful and then different for everybody?"

"Talley, when my mama says it's a wonderful day, do you see the same wonderful day that she sees?"

"Yeah," Talley said, after thinking a moment. "Probably do. Your mama and me see alike."

Didi sighed. "No, it has to be different for everybody because everybody's different," she said. "Each guy and each girl, their personalities are a different combination."

"But sex is sex," Talley murmured. "Wonderful is wonderful."

They were breathing hard and long now. They were flat out, pulling, running with speed.

"Un-uh," Didi said. "If you think that . . . Talley, don't do it."

"I wouldn't!"

"You will, someday."

"Nobody's going to love me."

"What's love got to do wit' it!" Didi sang out and laughed a phony, hard and tough sound deep in her throat.

Talley knew she didn't mean that, the way she'd mouthed off the famous lyrics to the Tina song. She knew that for Didi, love had everything to do with it.

Didi was teasing her, playing tough. Well, she could play right back. Guys played tough and macho all the time.

"You a witch, girl," Talley said, sounding bad. "Make me so sick, sometimes. You think you so cool."

A White Romance flashed before her eyes. She just knew AWR had to be same outta-sight magnificent-wonderful for everybody who saw it happen.

Chapter
SIX

Seemed that when she woke up Talley knew the day when it happened was going to be wonderful. Of course, she didn't know AWR was coming down just that day. But she had rolled out of a hideous dream. Excitement was part of the dream just as was the really awful.

She had been in this big room, with beds lined up. Students, sleeping. It was a sound-sleep room and she seemed to know that it was. Like a hotel where all of them went to sleep. That didn't seem odd or strange. On the wall above her bed was a round hole like a mouse hole, only larger. She was standing there, ready to get into the bed. A pleasant thought, to stretch herself out in bed and fall asleep. The only place she was allowed to sleep was in the sleep room.

Seemed there was conversation in the room. And tweetering. Talley heard the talking behind her somewhere and all around. She didn't mind it. The tweetering was not awfully annoying but it made her jittery. It wasn't loud; she didn't take the time to dwell on it. She was looking at the hole in the wall above her bed. There

58

was something in it, as there was in other holes above other beds. A bat. The bat was looking at her. It tweetered at her. It was a hairless bat. She could see its bare pointed ears and its teeth. It acted like it would spit at her but it didn't. It twitched its nose at her and then paid no more attention to her.

Seemed that in the dreaming, she went to bed, woke up, and it was the next morning. She kicked the covers down. Her legs suddenly hurt her. When she looked they were bleeding. There were teeth marks and gashes with dried blood around them.

Ooooh, the bat has bit me, she thought. I'm going to get sick!

She tried not to panic. She told somebody. And somebody said, "S'what happens when you sleep in the beds. These are sucking bats. By morning, they go back into their holes." Sure enough, the bats were in the holes again.

Seemed she couldn't bear the thought of a bat sucking her blood out while she slept. But it had happened. She got up, found a bucket that belonged to her. In the bottom of the bucket was her dark red blood. She emptied the bucket so she wouldn't see it anymore. Then, it was all clean. Her bucket looked brand new out of a store.

"We have to get some cement, seal up my hole in the wall," she said in the dream, to whoever it was behind her. She couldn't see. It was a guy, a friend. He seemed to understand. He said they would get some cement, seal up the hole. "Good," she told him. She leaned her head against him, closed her eyes. She got lost in a corridor to other rooms. He helped her find her way out of the place of rooms and beds. She held tightly to his hand, as though he were some father. Then, he hugged her.

Talley rolled out of the dream. "Wow," she said. She

was wide-awake, getting up. Stretching. "Who was the guy? Oooh, I hate bats! Why'd I dream about them?" She made a farfetched connection to the day before when she and this Didi Adair had been out running. They'd seen what was practically a flying squirrel going from tree to tree. They'd only been running together a couple of days. They'd both of them stopped in their tracks when they saw the squirrel leap. Its glide was unreal, it was so smooth.

"Wow!" Didi had said. "Did you see that?"

"Sure!" Talley said. "Never saw one do like that, though. You suppose they learn how to do that from their mamas, or are they born doing it?"

"Don't know," Didi said. The squirrel had little pointy ears.

And she and Didi had run some more. The nightmare had reminded her of running and the squirrel.

So that was when she'd begun to know this funny, be-white girl. They'd got together to run. Didi Adair was straight for-real beautiful-looking. Sometimes, Talley stole sidelong glances at her.

Everything about Didi was class and rich, was what Talley believed at first. Except that sometimes she would talk like a be-white from the Street, hanging out. Talked tough. It would take Talley a while to realize it was mostly put-on. Defensive.

She didn't know when she noticed, but from the beginning, circling Didi all the time was this be-white dude dressed in leather. You couldn't miss him, once you made the connection. It took Talley a while to put two and two together. But whenever you saw Didi Adair in the school halls, in the lunchroom, in study halls, you would see this guy the next minute, either following her or coming in the other direction. Kid was exotic-looking.

Real dirty-blond handsome. Really pale, though. Looking like a comic-book hero with the flu. A hero that was Didi's satellite.

Well, it wasn't her business, Talley thought. She and Didi just ran together still. They would meet after school. One of them would say, "You ready?" And the other would say, "Sure, I'm ready." Everybody see them. It made "race" relations have a double meaning. Race relations got better quicker in the Colonel Glenn, Talley liked to think. If Didi thought about race and civil rights and stuff, she never let on in the beginning before Talley met her mom. Didi was real cool and casual. Like nothing was different for her at all. Didi didn't care what color person floated around. Or what integrated big magnet she found herself enrolled in, she acted like. And then, they'd run together.

One day, early on, she said to Didi, "Who the dude? Who your be-white/satellite?" Real smart like that. Poem.

"Huh?" Didi said.

"You don't know?" Talley answered. "The guy hangs after you like a sick puppy! Real sharp clothes, leather and stuff. Expensive shades. He wears a studded wrist band like a *bandit*. Like a motorcycle dude." She didn't know then that heavy-metal dudes also wore wrist bands like that.

"Huh? Where! In school?" Didi had asked. They'd been running hard and they slowed down the pace.

"Girl! You're putting me on."

"No! What are you talking about?" Didi said.

"You don't know. You haven't seen nuth-thin! And the dude so close to you all the time, I thought he was talking to you. I thought you guys were going out and stuff."

"Nuh-uh," Didi said. "You sure he's scoping on me?"

"Girl, it's as plain as day."

"Well, I'll have to see, then," Didi said. "I think I know the one you mean!"

They'd laughed together. But Talley had wondered then about Didi. Did she *know* stuff about guys? She laughed like she did. Talley played tough but the home boys were onto her. Should she let Didi know she was only playing? Little Roxanne.

But that was the beginning. When AWR was born.

Then one day, change of classes. Who knew that this day would be the one! Buzzers sounded. Somebody, AP on the loudspeaker. Calling out names of kids to report to the office. The trigonomics teacher wouldn't be in; there would be a substitute. Stuff like that. Locker doors banging all up and down the halls. Students talking, laughing, complaining, jiving and woofing. School was like a busy city. Young adults moving fast; moving slow. Working at one another. Signifying, scoping, all things high-school students will do in the minutes they have with one another free and easy between classes. It was a new school and exciting. It was as if nothing existed but themselves. They were there for one another only, and what they saw, heard, cared about. It was early on. Tension, graffiti, but no real bad scenes yet.

All of a sudden, there was the be-blond handsome dude. Just there, out of nowhere, as soon as Talley saw Didi opening her locker. Didi Adair, superfine. She would always be most like a storybook princess whenever Talley came on her all of a sudden in the hall.

Didi wore a white angora sweater that crossed her heart and opened into a modified V neck. It was gathered at the waist with two gold waist buttons on the side for decoration. White angora that drove dudes wild once Didi, full front, was inside it. Sometimes, she wore a

sports bra, especially when out running. Now, under the angora, she hadn't worn anything.

She had on black designer jeans she must've melted and poured on. She had perfect runner's hips, which was to say she had very little. And the black jean fabric ran up her legs and over her flat belly and round behind without a crease. She was boyish from the waist down and an awful lot of girl under the angora. Her face: a star is born, all over it. Her hair, long and blow-fine. Clear, pink-skin-face thoughts behind clear gray-blue eyes. She had a mouth, nose, eyes, lips, cheeks like everybody. But all hers came together with ease. In perfect beauty. All that sex all over her seemed to fill up her face with tenderness.

Didi had it all, Talley was thinking. Students pushed by her. Talley stood there watching this new girl in her old school—new magnet—she was now running with. Be-white beauty.

When all at once, this dude wearing a leather body-suit enclosed Didi. Where'd he come from? Came out of nowhere. Leather jacket and leather pants. Must've cost three, four hundred dollars, the whole outfit. He surrounded Didi. He enveloped her, enfolded her without so much as a word of warning. Talley saw it all. Saw Didi's face seem to fill with this look Talley hadn't seen come over her before. Well, she hadn't known the girl too long. But it was some kind of caring, Jim.

Girl knows this guy now! Talley had time to think. Just that look of intense, delirious concentration told her that leather dude and Didi had got together. They must've been out together since Talley had told Didi about him circling her.

Talley, down the hall a short distance at her own locker. When she turned, she looked left over at them.

63

She saw the whole thing. Watching, grinning all over her face.

Couldn't believe what was going down. Talley saw Didi's notebooks seem to float to the floor as the dude took hold of her. Seemed so loud, the notebooks falling with pages flapping, like in slo-mo through the air.

Amusing! Bet he's going to give her a soul kiss . . . A-may-zing!

She froze against her locker. Couldn't believe what she was seeing. The leather dude had cupped his hands over the angora, over Didi braless, closing and opening his hands.

Goo-ood night!

Didi was slanted half inside her own locker like she intended to lie in it. She'd backed away from the dude, who was now on her like snow on ice, melting. Then, his mouth was on hers. He was kissing her, all right. He ate Didi's mouth, it seemed like. His wide-open mouth covered half her face. Clear up under her nose. His eyes were closed. His hands moving down the angora, all down over Didi's no-hips.

The hallway hushed, like someone had announced a pin dropping and they all had to listen to it. Like, they heard it, too. Well, they couldn't help noticing this gorgeous chick and this leather dude Prince Charming, both tall, lean pales, shooting a scene right before their eyes.

Seconds of silence as they watched, the dude's head had made it inside the locker. His shoulders about blocked the view inside but Talley could see his hands were gone behind Didi's back somewhere. You could see part of Didi, her upper torso. See part of her chin. He was lifting her up along the leather as high as his waist. She was up his body, no two ways about it. Talley saw it all.

Didi's hands crawled around his neck and up the back of his hair, ruffling it in the sweetest move. And holding his head in her arms, her elbows sticking out of the locker in the air like pale wings. Dude, moving with Didi. Something so secret. Stunning, shocking, weren't *even* the words for it.

There was sudden noise. Homes and dudes whooped and hollered up and down the long corridor. And cries of "Shhhh! Shhhhh, y'all!" Others were saying things that were loud, frank and rank. The girls half-turned away— "What do they think they're *doing!*" "Oh, my goodness . . . they are going to get in trouuu-ble. . . ."

Some be-black girls looked grim. "S'what happens when They in The Neighborhood. Offensive! My mama hear about that kinda stuff, she taken me on outta here, too."

"Honey, who's going to tell your mama some-thin? And where else you going to go?"

Talley looked away more than once but she was unable to keep her eyes off the dude and Didi. Couldn't help looking and seeing. Her insides were mushy; nerves, jumping.

Didi was backed inside the locker. All Talley could think was that the leather dude had to be hurting her. Harsh movements.

Going to get her in some mess, too, she thought. But then she saw Didi's hands on the dude's hair. She hadn't ever noticed them just that way before. Just by themselves. Hands, like bright flowers; like white lily petals.

Ever after when she recalled the time in the hall, she would see Didi's pale fingers. Of lilies, so still. Then, fluttering, as in a light breeze on a pond somewhere. Just for a second, then the breeze would disappear. So romantic! Lilies. White and still.

The noise was loud around Talley. Banging lockers. Homes, overreacting, urging the dude on, signifying— "Put it, put-put, put-out! Knock it, put it, put-out!"

It's a white romance, Talley found herself thinking. That dude and Didi. "Hey, hey, hey!" Talley heard herself. She was clapping—it was so—wow! "A white romance!" She yelled it, delighted by the beauty of lilies and love. Some heard her. She'd turned the other way to include everybody in the hall—"A White Romance!"— and so, was first to see the authority coming.

They all were tuned to authority. It played in the background of their lives like static on the radio. They tuned it in or out, depending. And they could even see it coming almost before it came.

Talley saw it first, that polished and shined shoe; pants leg, dark fall wool, coming around the corner. Mr. Judd. The instant she saw the one leg before the other she began to shout it loud and rowdy: "Hey, hey, what I say! There go a white romance, Jim. There go *A White Romance!* Oooh-hooo!" And pointing down the hall past the AP, who was about to turn the corner, toward her, when he paused and looked the other way.

"What? Where!" Others, coming to their lockers, took it up.

Long enough. While the guys were closing in around the leather dude and Didi's business that was still going on. Leather out in a world of Didi Adair.

All happening so fast! Give Didi time, at least to get out of the hall, Talley was thinking. Get her out of some mess.

"Hey, man, cut it!" one of the guys said. The leather dude and Didi were surrounded by other guys, even some homes, trying to get them apart. "I'm gittin' my own self outta here," a home said, and cut out.

They had got the leather dude away from the locker but he wasn't letting Didi go. He sat down right in the corridor with her cradled in his arms. His back was up against the lockers. He still kissed her.

They're not like kids, Talley was thinking. Didi's hands in his hair. Right before her eyes it was like a real grown-up romance.

Some girls were yelping in fear and chirping half with delight. Flinging themselves up against closed lockers all up and down the corridor, aroused.

"What's he think he's *doing—in-sane!*"

The AP wasn't to be fooled by Talley hollering. He was running toward Didi and the leather dude. Talley tried once more, like she was playing on somebody: "Oooh, here come *A White Romance!*" She didn't know how else to warn them. She couldn't say it straight out that the AP was coming—*y'all cool it!* so she said, "Here come . . . you all . . . A White Romance!" Mixing up words and thoughts. Meaning, stop it, the *authority* is here.

Somebody touched her on her shoulder. Gently squeezed it. "Hush, Talley," spoken calmly, as whoever it was went by her. It was Victor.

Victor, to help cool everybody. She caught a whiff of his cologne. Nice.

Other kids had taken it up: "A white romance!"

"A white romance, what? Where! Oh!"

"Talley, woofing on somebody, that's all. See? A white romance. Look at *them!*"

"Mercy!"

"Be still, y'all," Victor told them, smacking heads lightly left and right. He was with his be-white counterpart, Stuart, who did the same.

"Who, you?" some said, but not too loudly. You did not sass the Council guys. Nor the AP, who was pushing kids away and telling them to move along down the long corridor.

But Talley's words stuck in their minds—Didi and the leather dude, A White Romance. Victor tried to make the leather dude get up. Leather held Didi tightly, and he wasn't getting up or letting go. A White Romance!

"In trouuu-ble!" Somebody screamed it. Talley flattened against her locker as students rushed every which way.

"Halt! Stop that running. Halt! Everybody stay in place!" hollered Mr. Judd.

Why'd somebody have to scream? A wave of fear flowed over Talley. She hoped she wouldn't be noticed.

Kids slowed but they didn't stop. Dudes walked away from the leather dude and Didi. Homes slid by and out.

There were two more teachers in the hall.

Everything! Talley thought, shaking from excitement at what she'd seen. But finally, she moved, opened her locker, took out the books she needed and put others back. Her movements, jerky, shot through with nerves. Everything coming down on Didi now.

She turned away from her newfound friend. Too dawn late. A very doomed White Romance! She saw the AP, with strong Victor's and Stuart's help, wrench the dude by the collar and up. Slam the dude against the lockers. Call for Security. They would search the leather dude and then his locker. Show their authority.

Talley saw the leather dude give Didi one sad, soulful look as the two women teachers jerked her to her feet and marched her toward the administration offices.

You see her hands were lilies? All fluttery and sweet? Just about as tender as anything. Just like some calla lilies. Why they have to go crush her like that?

Ever after for Talley, shaped in Didi's caressing

hands—something alive with desire. Maybe R-rated. But it wasn't bad. It was Didi Adair looking up at this dude— soon Talley would know he was Roady—and being bathed in some passion, Jim, in some caring. Bathed in sunlight. It was the dude touching Didi, not to be *rude.*

Touching like that. Ooooh!

But because he had to, he couldn't help himself. It was the two of them together, the way Talley was sure it would never happen with her and somebody.

What do I know? she thought. Maybe I was meant to be a loner. There was something appealing about the picture she had then. Her forlorn self, wandering the earth forever with just the sound of her footsteps for company. Sunsets, walking into them, slowly, sadly.

But it was too dawn perfect. Too outta-sight wonderful. AWR.

Chapter
SEVEN

Everybody knew when the parents came to school. It was the day after AWR came down. This man had come. It had taken a while for everybody to connect the slim, handsome, very what-you-call-it, ele-gawnt man in his Burberry raincoat with the sharp plaid lining, to AWR and young leather dude. But *the man* turned out to be leather's "old man"—G. D. Lewis, initials for Gregory Dean. And the leather dude's name was, of course, Roady Lewis, with Dean his middle name as well. Roady Dean Lewis.

That's when everybody found out that Mr. G. D. and Roady were not on very good speaking terms. Well, word gets around. You can't keep any secrets with secretaries and assistants and student office aides in the outer offices. Students will find out what they think is their business, one way or another.

G. D. Lewis relayed whatever he had to say to Roady Dean through the AP or a secretary or whatever kid assistant was handy. "Tell the boy that his mother wants him to call her." Or "Tell the boy I don't want to hear of this ever happening again. It will make sense to him coming from one of you."

Karyn Smith told Talley, "And Roady right here, not two feet away from his own dad. And G. D. acting like he not there. Can you believe it?"

Karyn was an aide, doing some of the typing and filing twelve hours a week. G. D., ordering everybody around and not even aware he was doing it, he was so used to doing it, Karyn said. Like they were all his servants, and everybody jumping, even the AP, like they thought they were his servants, too. Always, G. D. said "the boy" for Roady's real name.

Karyn told Talley and a bunch of other girls everything over lunch in the lunchroom. "Can you dig it? The old dude rides up in a black English *Jag*. An XJ6. And double-parks it right in front of the school. And dares anybody to dent a fender. *Dares*. I saw Billy Jay turn into the street in his little Mustang. He see the Jag and didn't even try it. He back on out of there, too."

Students in the offices realized soon enough that G. D. Lewis was a downright evil man. He gave Roady plenty of money, paid all his bills.

"Anybody *nice* know you keep a space cadet on a short lifeline. You don't go giving him a mellow, spaceship ride. You don't be giving him a free, suicide ticket on a silver platter. No way," Karyn said.

But he's not a space cadet, not completely, Talley thought. And maybe that was why all the kids grew to like Roady so much. There was something through all the empty space in his head that was sane and straight and kind of sweet. And they realized early on that the old man, G. D., couldn't stand him. Even the teachers were sympathetic to Roady, finally, seeing the kind of pressure he was under from his G. D. dad.

71

It was easy to understand how Didi's mom, Vera Adair, got lost in the shuffle. That is, she wasn't noticed because G. D. Lewis was such a scene. Talley didn't meet Mrs. Adair until later, when she was going over to Didi's all the time.

The school had thought to expel Didi and Roady Lewis for good. But pressure from Roady's dad changed the thinking. And both Roady and Didi were transfers to the Magnet with good records.

"Everybody saying that Roady and Didi ain't see *nobody* but each other from the minute they walk in the offices," Karyn told them. "They looking straight into each other's eyes. And nothing anybody going to do ain't changed the fact that the two of them together can stop silver bullets, Jim. A tank roll right oveh them and they get up, still huggin' and kissin'. A White Romance!"

Everybody laughed their heads off at this last. Everybody except Talley. She had seen the way Roady and Didi looked into each other's eyes. She knew how it must be for them feeling so deeply for one another like that.

The principal didn't want any kind of "adverse" publicity. So the school would find ways they could "modify" the behavior of these two students "with great potential"; and therefore, "neutralize" the "difficulty."

Students working in the offices more than a week began to sound just like some assistant principal. Parents were called in, said Karyn, to "assist" the school in "determining" the "proper discipline" for a "student offender's" particular "offense."

"In other words . . ." Talley had said to Karyn.

"In other words," Karyn had answered, "A White Romance be sleeping home in bed till noon for a week. That's called suspension from classes because they be acting like dum-basses. But after that, they cool. They can come on back in. Ain't it nice to be rich and do whatever you want, and in love, too!"

"Must be something," Talley had murmured.

Now, still running with Didi, she almost said it out loud—"Must be something," so caught was she in the memory of AWR. "You can be thinking on something, and you won't know how you got to where you are," she murmured.

"Well, we're here, cookie-face," Didi said, "and here comes the bus."

"I see it is," Talley said. It was the only city bus that went all the way out to Didi's house and a few blocks beyond from Roady's part of town. It usually took them thirty minutes from curb to curb.

Talley was glad the bus had come. The drizzling rain had changed to something heavier. "In another minute, we'd be soaked," she said, as the bus pulled up. Sleek sound, tires on the wet pavement. That sighing as the doors opened.

They got on. Didi paid and Talley gave the driver her transfer. Bus was a third full.

How they run buses when they can't get people to ride them? she wondered. Poppy say that when the buses go by always on this side of empty, you know folks is out of work. He's probably right about that.

They sat down on the last seat of the bus—the long cross seat—right in the middle. A guy half-asleep had the window seat in one corner. Talley looked him over, in a quick appraisal. He really did look tired. She gave him one of her swift judgments. No trouble. But she kept him in the back of her mind. You always remembered who was near you, so that when you got off, you could remember and know if they got off at the same place. There was a woman with shopping bags and a little girl at the other window. Talley didn't bother to remember them for longer than a few seconds. The little girl was kicking her legs up and down to show off what looked like new tennis shoes.

Talley took out a scarf from her bookbag and pulled it over her hair. She tied it under her hair at the nape of her neck.

"I'm going to catch me a cold out here," she said to Didi.

"You always think you will but you never do," Didi said. "I can't remember when you've had even a sniffle."

"You, either," Talley said. "But Roady be sniffling all the time."

Didi looked away out of the window. "You're so bloody American!" she said, out of the side of her mouth.

"What's that supposed to mean? American? I am American. So?"

"Forget it," Didi said.

"Look, if you don't want me to come home with you, I'll get off at the next stop."

"Oh, come on!"

"Well, I don't get you sometimes," Talley said. One minute, they were just talking and the next minute, something happened. Maybe that was the way sisters were. But she wouldn't know, not having any. Or brothers, either.

Bet if I had a sister or brother, I'd understand kids better, she thought. Sometimes, she felt out of it, not understanding half of what went on around her. Or what she thought might be going on around her. She never knew for sure.

"Did I say something about Roady?"

"No! Just forget it."

"Well, you don't have to be so mean . . ."

74

"I'm not mean—Talley, we ran over three miles."

"That's nothing."

"In the rain!"

"I love the rain!" Talley said.

"I *hate* it!" Didi said.

"That's because when it rain, even a little wave fall out your hair." Talley giggled a low sound in her throat.

"You are so stupid, sometimes," Didi said.

"Wet blow-hair smell like chicken feathers, and dead straight, too." And she laughed again.

"That just the conditioner I used. That's what you smell."

"Whatevah," Talley giggled.

"I wouldn't talk about your hair," Didi said, "'cause you couldn't take it."

Talley sobered at once, shot Didi a look.

"See what I mean? You're overly sensitive about your hair, that's why you cover it up from the rain."

"People look at it kinking up."

"It *curls*, Talley. Think of it that way. It's the way you think about it. So let people look. What do you care."

"But they looking at me with an *attitude*."

"So now you worry about what's in people heads? You can read their minds?" Didi asked.

"I can tell by their expressions. Their eyes."

"Yeah? Well, maybe so. But what's in their heads is their problem."

"It's mine, too, when they got the power to make me look stupid," Talley said.

"Only when you let them get to you. And who out here's got any power, for heaven's sake!"

"Boring, Didi."

"So. You started it. All the time talking about my hair.

75

Like I had something to do with it. We both born how we're born."

Talley had no answer because that was the truth. She closed her eyes a moment.

The sighing bus doors, opening and closing. Somebody brought the rain in close to them. Sat down on the right-hand side seats next to them. She would've dozed off if Didi hadn't started talking.

"Where you going now?"

"Got some business *out*," a male voice answered.

She's talking to someone, Talley thought.

"Better keep it out, too," Didi said.

"Hey. Who's your friend?"

"Can't tell, it's a secret," Didi said. "Hey, how did you know she's with me? Huh?"

Talking about *me*.

"Took a lucky guess."

That voice . . .

Talley had heard the voice before. She opened her eyes just enough to see.

"Peekaboo," said the guy. He was leaning toward her, hands deep in the pockets of his sleek leather jacket. Her eyes shot all the way open. It was Mr. Blow-hair, himself. Hair, brown and blondish, cut short and spiky in front and long on the sides and the back. It was the dude who had been at the door of Roady's building when she rang the buzzer. Now, he had a silver bookbag slung over one shoulder.

Smiling at her. Eyes, following her glance to the bookbag. "Hi-ho, Silver!" he murmured. Gleaming, straight teeth. "Just call me The Lone Shif'less. I got a white horse named Flying Home. Anytime you want, we'll take you for a riiiide!"

"You're disgusting and very boring," Didi said to him.

76

Him? Boring? Everything he said was somehow exciting to Talley. She sat up, pretended she'd been sleeping.
Stretched. Maybe she had been dozing. She sure must've
missed something. What was he talking about?

He waved at her, both hands waving frantically, although they were no more than two feet apart.

"Roxanne," he said, softly, like a purr. "Well, hey! We
haven't been properly introduced."

"Don't tell him who you are," Didi warned.

Talley looked at her. Was she kidding? She wasn't kidding. She didn't give Talley any clear signal.

He already knows my real name, Talley thought. He
winked at her. She smiled at him. You remember me, at
Roady's building? she wanted to say to him but didn't.
Saying that would've put them together somehow.

Glancing at Didi again, something about her face was
like a mask. Talley wondered what was the matter.

The dude leaned over and poked Didi in the shoulder.
"*We* haven't been properly introduced, I said," he said to
her. Knuckles pressed into her shoulder.

Didi's face turned red. At once she said, "This is
David."

The dude kept up the pressure. Talley could imagine
that he was hurting Didi. Guys never realized how strong
they were. Oh, but he was great-looking!

"David Emory," Didi said. "This is Talley." Spoken
quickly.

"Well, hey, Talley," he said and winked at her again,
like they had a big secret. He did have a fan-tastic smile,
lit up his eyes. Brown eyes. He took his knuckles away
from Didi. Caught hold of Talley's hand, leaning toward
her. They shook hands. He wouldn't let go. The heat of
his palm against her own shot up her arm, it felt like.
Made her stir inside.

"Hey, Talley, what? I don't know your last name," he said, squeezing her hand, then easing the pressure in a slow, feeling motion.

Made her want to melt down. "Talley Barbour," she managed. Didi said her last name, too, like an echo.

"Oh, hi!" he said, acting astonished to know Talley. She couldn't tell if he was kidding with her or not. Bewhite could act enthusiastic like that sometimes. But he was really one good-looking blow-hair.

"Hi," she said. "You're Roady's friend."

"That's right. We met earlier this evening." He turned to Didi. "Surprise! I already met her."

"No kidding. Big stupid deal, too," Didi said.

"Look at me, sweets," he said right back to her. "Don't be staring out the window when I'm talking to you. Or I'll have to take it up with Roady, and you wouldn't want that. Good old Roady," he said, smiling at her.

Didi's face turned pale. Her baby-blue-gray eyes were bright with sparks.

"What's the matter with you, girl?" Talley asked.

"I'm tired, is all," Didi said, softly.

"She's tired, is all," David said.

He looked up under his brows at Talley. Prettiest brown eyes. I thought they were lighter before, she thought. How come I thought that? "You still got my *hand!*" she squealed, grinning at him. "Man, let go!"

"Heyyyy. . . . Got a smile," he said, and then: "Where you going, way out here?"

"Over to Didi's." She pulled her hand away.

"Over to Didi's," he repeated. "Well, hey, mind if I tag along?"

Talley tried to signal Didi to let David Emory tag along.

Didi pressed her lips together. Said, "Mom has dinner

". . . and Talley and I have papers to write . . ." She let her eyes grow big at Talley, saying "no" in warning.

Talley tried to hide her disappointment.

"Hey, some other time, then," he said to her, bobbing his head, nodding at her to agree.

Talley smiled uncertainly.

"Dimples!" he said. "Did anybody ever tell you you're as cute as a kitten?"

"No!" she said, and couldn't help giggling.

"No. You're cuter than a pussycat. Hey, you're a cute little fox, Roxanne."

"Don't call me that!"

"Fox? Or Roxanne?" he laughed at her.

She couldn't help laughing too. Forgot all about Didi for a minute.

"Maybe I'll stop back after you're finished," he told Talley.

Right on that, Didi said, "Her dad comes at ten to pick her up." A shocking lie.

Like I'm some little kid! Talley thought. She felt her face burn hot.

"Oh, your dad comes to pick you up? I don't blame him, way out here with the riffraff." He glanced smiling at Didi. His eyes were wise, as if he knew Talley's dad didn't pick her up. Like Didi, herself, was the riffraff.

"What's your dad's name?" he said to Talley.

"Hale William Barbour," she said.

"What's he do?"

"You got a lot of questions," Didi said.

"You're making me sick," the dude said, right back to her. He didn't bother even to look at her. He smiled at Talley and talked about Didi as if she weren't

79

there. "She and I used to date some. But she was too jealous."

"That's a lie and you know it! Who'd wanta be jealous of you?" Didi said.

David laughed. "She'd always say, 'Did you look at that girl? I saw you looking at that other one.' All the time she was worried I was looking. Hey, I was! Man, what else is there to do?"

"Wh-what, really? You guys?" Talley said, looking at Didi anew. "Then you all knew one another before the Magnet. Roady, too?"

"No," Didi said.

"Just her and me," David said. "We come from the same part of town. My folks still live out here. I got lots of . . . cli . . . friends out here. What's your dad do?" he asked again. "Probably as little as possible!" He laughed. "No, just kidding!"

"He works hard!" Talley said, indignantly. "He's the caretaker for three of the closed plants," said more calmly. "He does the best job of anybody."

"You mean, he's the night watchman," David said. "Say it like it is."

"Officially, though, he's the caretaker."

"He works at night, though," the dude murmured. His eyes on her lips, down her neck.

"Yeah, of course," Talley said, looking away, as his eyes traveled.

The dude was on his feet. Talley realized the bus was coming to a stop. He touched Talley's knee, looked into her eyes. "Well, hey!" he said.

"Well, hey, yourself!" she said right back.

"Later," he said, grinning, enclosing her in a last, perfect smile.

He was all motion and energy, like a cat, a panther,

flowing off the bus. Gone that fast, with the scent of his after-shave and his body heat mixed in her nostrils. She took a deep breath. She felt dizzy. That quick, she'd forgotten what he looked like, exactly. Hadn't had the time to fix him in her mind. But she knew he was gorgeous. That, she was sure of.

Chapter
EIGHT

"**M**an-oh-man. Dude is something. David Emory. That's a nice name."

"He thinks he's Hollywood and he ain't for nothing," Didi said.

"You saying that just because he seems like he's coming on to me."

"No, I'm not, Talley. I'm just saying what he is. He's sorry as he can be," Didi said. "David Emory would be a joke if he wasn't an absolute zero to begin with."

"You ever see zero looking like that, or dress like that? Or have manners like that?" Talley asked her. "I think he's got a great personality."

Didi stared at her. "I'm not talking about his *personality*. I don't believe you sometimes, girl. Don't you know . . . ? No, I can see you don't."

"Don't I know what? Tell me, what were you going to say?" Talley pleaded.

"Just . . ." Didi shook her head. Sighed. "Talley . . . well, you know what your dad will do if you mess with somebody, a white dude."

Talley didn't say anything at first. "I'm not messing with him," she said, finally. "I was just talking to him. Anyway. Poppy don't know nothing about it. He didn't *see* me. Didi, maybe you are just a little bit jealous David Emory is looking at me, too."

"I don't *believe* you."

"I mean, you did date him, go with him. Maybe you still feel for him."

"I'm with Roady and you know it."

"So? Maybe you are still jealous." Talley felt hateful saying that, but she went ahead and said it anyway.

"You're wrong," Didi said. "But I'll butt out. It sure ain't my business."

"You right about that," Talley said. She felt sure of herself. On Didi's level. They'd never really had guys to talk about before or to fight over.

To think a guy who once liked Didi was playing at *her*, talking to *her*.

This is where you find out who your friends really are, Talley realized. She didn't dare fantasize about herself and the dude. For-get *it*! Don't even think *it*.

Didi stared out of the window, half-turned away from Talley. Arms tightly folded.

"You not going to talk to me?" Talley said after a minute. "Sitting like that, all mad and stuff . . ."

"I'm not mad. I've just . . . got nothing to say," Didi mumbled.

"Fine. You rather I didn't come over your house, I won't," Talley said. She stared hard at her friend. She really wanted to come over. Her evenings by herself could be long and boring. Poppy didn't like her to have girls over. *"They ain't into nothing but gossip. They sure not into studying books. What good they going to do you, young lady? Don't even think about having some cat off the street over."*

83

She was almost never alone in the evenings since she and Didi had been friends. They went over to Didi's after Didi finished at Roady's. And Mrs. Adair usually made Talley have a little supper with them. Talley had offered to pay in the beginning. But Mrs. Adair wouldn't hear of it.

"She's gone clear goofy about you," Didi had told Talley. "My mom really thinks you two were related in some former life. I mean it."

Talley was sure of it. She and Mrs. Adair got along so well. *"Honey, put your head on my shoulder awhile. Let Didi stay on the phone all night. Didi's older than I am, I swear to you. I don't have a baby anymore. She was grown up by the time she started first grade. Put your head down, that's it, and I'll be your stepmama—how's that? Did I tell you what it was like when I was a child? Oh, my father was strict! He allowed no back talk! We came to America when I was two. We ate a lot of bread and potatoes on the long crossing. You think I was too little to remember. I do remember. You ate heavy so the food would stay down. My papa insisted on that. 'Eat, baby, eat.' So I ate. Oh, some people were deathly sick. Not me, never.*

"Didi's like me. I was born older. Well, some things you can't forget. Believe me, you girls have it easy.

"My mother wasn't well, so I kept house for my daddy and her, once we were in Brooklyn, America. I went to school at night. In those days, you paid your own way. I sold candy in the subway stations. I made a few dimes that way. Long days and nights. But I was pretty and alive and who needed to sleep? By the time I was sixteen, I was married. Divorced at eighteen. Oh, I suppose I was wild. Didi's like me, I can't say a word. But that was the way it

was then, if you were pretty. You could find somebody else. I did, but not for a while."

She'd have her forehead against Vera Adair's smooth jaw and her arm draped over her plump shoulder. She'd have her eyes closed and she didn't have to talk if she didn't want to. Mrs. Adair would just go on and on, with Talley grunting now and then, or occasionally, lifting her head to ask a dumb question.

Talley realized she was still sitting there on the bus, waiting for Didi to answer her. She'd been thinking so hard. Swiftly, it came to her, what she loved about going over to the Adair house. Oh, she cared about Didi. But she guessed she was jealous of her in a way. Jealous of her looks, of her and Roady. She loved Mrs. Adair with no reservations. Loved listening to her and feeling so relaxed with her. She never thought about their different colors at all, not since the beginning, until now. She was close to Mrs. Adair, Vera, and she be-white. So how was it so different with a David Emory?

"I got to pick up some things for Roady at the drugstore," Didi said. Abruptly she was on her feet and walking down the bus aisle.

The bus came to a stop. Hey, wait . . . Talley wanted to call out to Didi. She wanted to go with her. But now, she didn't feel free. Didi's every move told how she didn't want to be bothered with Talley this evening. Not once did she look back before she swung out of the door.

Well. I won't go where I'm not wanted. Talley sighed. Swallowed a couple of times. Now she really was alone.

What got into Didi, anyhow? Was it really the boy, David? There was something there with her and him. I got to play it back tonight and study it. I'll go over everything once I get home. First, I got to get home.

Now she would have to go to the end of the bus line. It can't be far, she thought. The next stop is the one Didi and I usually get off at. And after that is the end of the line, somewhere. And the bus turns around.

The bus started up and she felt awful inside. Didi, her friend. Well, now you got no friend, I mean, a real close one. What do you think of that?

How come you have to say everything comes in your head? Maybe I'm the one is jealous 'cause I don't got nobody like Roady.

Who'd want somebody like him? Some smoking pill-popper, and worse.

I could go out with lots of guys, but they'd never get past Poppy. Glad I got Poppy. She don't got a dad she'd want to know, Mrs. Adair says.

I didn't do nothing. All I said was the truth. She was jealous, that was it. She was upset that the dude, David, was paying attention to me. What else could it be? I mean, maybe I'm better-looking than I thought. Guys look at me all of the time. But then, they scope on everybody. She wants them all to just scope on her? No way, Jim. Always putting myself down. Shoot. I'm all right. So I'm short, be-black, so what? Poppy calls me petite, a young lady, too. I'm as good as anybody come over in steerage.

Leave *her* out of it. She's a nice lady, been like a mother to me.

"The next man I married and the only man I married after the first ne'er-do-well. Talley, do you know what is meant by a ne'er-do-well? We found each other when I was thirty-five. We went together a long time. He wanted to move inland, he said. So we moved to Chicago. Wasn't Brooklyn, that's for sure. We married and left the east coast for 'inland.' I was thirty-seven by then. Had Didi

when I was forty—do you believe it? He was fifty. Fifty years old and tired to the bone. Well, I couldn't take it. The sound of him, the gray, squat look of him began to grate on my nerves. Honey, never marry just to marry. Wait for love, even when you guess it might not come. At least, you have a wish and you have faith.

"So I took my Didi and came here. Well, it's not so bad. I knew Didi would be all right from the time I got the flu when she was five and she had to take care of me. She did! She found a box and stood on it to make me soup. It took her an hour to open the can. She had on my housecoat and it came down to the floor. I will never, ever forget what a skinny-looking little bit she was in that yellow housecoat.

"I couldn't get up to help her. All I could do was moan. But the child fed me and talked to me. Kissed my hair and kept me going. Now she takes care of Roady Dean. Well, I trust Didi. Some women have to nurse, don't ask me why. I'm glad she has faith."

With Mrs. Adair's voice running through her mind, it was as if Talley's insides emptied out and that forlorn feeling, that sad emptiness, came gliding in.

The bus driver asking her what for and where. She told him she would go to the end of the line and back. The bus was as empty now as she was.

"It don't make no sense," he said, suspicious of her riding back and forth.

"I forgot something. I don't have the right book to study at my friend's house. Might as well go on home." *If it's any your business.*

He shut up, then. The end of the line was where he got off. "The other fella will take your money," he said, and got off.

She sat on the bus with the door open and the motor

87

running. Dark out. They were at a corner where there was a drugstore. People were coming to get on. A few got on. The bus was no longer alone. She was, though. She moved clear over to the window to look out on the black, shining street. Street was wet, with water in a stream at the gutters. Tears came down the wide bus windows.

Oh, it's night and I'm by myself again. Thinking that, feeling sorry for herself made her feel a little better. A contradiction, but true. Why not feel sorry? And feel better for it? Was there anyone ever to feel sorry for her? Times like these, she thought she would be better off dead.

Feeling flat inside, she'd thought about what it would be like to kill herself.

Not the same as being dead!

Amused by the thought of taking her carry and cutting her wrists. She'd heard that when you cut your wrists, the veins jump out like long blue worms to squirt blood all over the room. Somebody once told her that it had happened to somebody else they knew.

Poppy would have to clean it up. Him cleaning her off the walls made her squirm there on the bus. I'd see my own blood all over the lampshade and curtains before I passed out.

Come on, get off it! she thought, as the new driver climbed onto the bus. Once he was settled, she followed others to put her fare in the money machine.

I'll be home for hours all alone.

After she sat down again, the ride didn't seem long. She had the blow-hair dude on her mind. When she closed her eyes, she couldn't see him, but felt his motion, his energy leaning toward her. His look, boring into her. Whatever words he'd said had mostly slipped her mind.

Why can't I remember anything? She was left with the shape of his voice inside her, pleasing her. The sound of a *guy.*

She was in The Neighborhood by ten o'clock. Old familiar, be-black town. She breathed a sigh of relief. On her street, she nodded at people whom she knew. Everybody hurried, after dark. A girl alone didn't tarry long. You didn't want a reputation of hanging out. Vultures after prey were always hanging out, too. And even though she had her carry where she could reach it in a second, she didn't want to become preyed upon. She ran home late when she was over to Didi's. This time she would be early. Usually, she got home an hour before Poppy did. He didn't know anything about that.

He'd kill me if he knew, too. But he don't know because he don't talk to people, working by himself and at night. He wouldn't talk to people even if he didn't work at night. Poppy is the most lone man there is on earth. Has to be. Kids in school say they seen "your daddy" places and he wasn't alone.

"You didn't see Poppy, shoot. He working so way late."

"Saw him, honey, and he working, all right. But not like you think. He got this lady, fine and tall. Who she be? Ain't from The Neighborhood, that's for sure."

Almost laughing at her because they thought they knew something she never even suspected.

"You must be mistaken, too. Wasn't Poppy. He don't got time for nobody." She could've added "but me" to the "for nobody." She didn't want them to crack up about it. Everybody thought she was a goody-two-shoes and didn't know anything.

She was in the apartment a little after ten. She could do what she had to do without even thinking about it. First she put her bookbag on the chair in the kitchen.

She got out of her running top and put on a long-sleeved shirt. She wiped her face and hair on a paper towel. But she really wasn't that wet. Her running shoes were wet and dirty. She kicked them off and took them into the bathroom. Ran water over them in the tub to clean them off. She wrapped them in a towel and took them to the dryer down the hall. She let them flop around inside. They'd be dry in an hour.

Then she got things ready for Poppy. Still not needing to concentrate her mind on what she was doing. She knew how to set the table, how to arrange everything on the table, and then take out her books, push her plate away, and lay her books out. So that it would look as if she'd been studying there for the whole evening. She worked on the English paper for about forty-five minutes. In the midst of that, she made chili in stages; first, the meat, then the beans and onions, chili powder and whole tomatoes. She had it all together in twenty minutes, and studying the whole time. Working out her English paper.

It was called "Say It Isn't So." She didn't know why it was called that. It just came to her. Before she knew it, she was writing the whole evening that had just happened.

Thinking, if Didi sees this, she's going to be mad at me. But she won't see it. I'll turn it in and she'll never see it.

She thought of changing the title to "Boy Meets Girl" but that sounded too young and silly. "Say It Isn't So" was about meeting this guy the girl in the story falls in love with but doesn't want to. In the story both the girl and the boy be-black. She decided the boy wouldn't like the girl and that's why the girl says, "Say it isn't so, Phery." The home's name was David McPherson. Everybody called him Phery.

"Pronounced, 'Furry,'" Talley murmured to herself.

Anytime she thought about people to write them down, she wrote about their color. She wished not to think of color all of the time but it seemed like she had to. There was no way not to.

Didi write something, she never once think about them be-white. I know she doesn't. Why should she? So why do I?

The frustration of having to say the skin colors of the couple in the story made her angry with herself. I don't *have* to say, she thought. I *think* I have to say.

If I told the real story, I'd have to say more than one color and I ain't ready to get involved with that! So why not take all the color out? What will happen if you do? Nobody's going to put a gun to your head, make you do it one way or the other. Do what you want to.

She concentrated on taking out all mention of color, including eye color. She wasn't going to comment on somebody having light eyes, even when they were light brown. And she found that what the couple talked about, what they thought about, and the way they lived, told their color clearly to most anyone.

There! Talley thought. You learned something tonight.

Wonder what that David Emory is doing. He's not feeding his dad, I bet. He's not even home yet, I bet. But what if he drops by Didi's later to find me, only I'm not there! Oh, dang it! What if he does? And there will be Didi just waiting for him! I don't care. I don't *care.* Why should I care about either one of them? They ain't my *kind.* Oh, I hate the whole thing. I just *hate* it.

She stretched across her books, her head on her arms. Closed her eyes.

Hate everybody and everything. Feeling so sad, so

empty, all of a sudden, for about the tenth time today. Poppy, come home and talk to me!

She fell asleep like that, across her books. The chili cooked slowly on the back of the stove. Soon, its aroma filled the kitchen.

Hale Barbour came in about twelve-thirty. Worry giving him the indigestion again. Actually, the pain was caused by the beer and peanuts he'd had over Rochella's house before coming home. He'd walked off the job early. Who was to know? He did his job, could walk off when he felt like it. Long as he let the two Dobermans loose at either end of the one plant property, he was all right. Nobody was going to come nosing. Don't let a soul know that Princer, the fastest and the one that could leap farthest, was a pansy. Give him cheese and he'd roll over every time.

Hale smelled the chili as he hit the landing. He felt the tension leave his body but the worry stayed with him. He dreaded coming home these times. He'd seen the changes coming over Talley. She was a good young lady. But she was curious like any bright student. Oh, the pitfalls along the way! He worried so that some random chance, being in the wrong place, might cause her damage, pain. Hurt her, his baby girl.

He worried about all the toughs and the lazies and no-accounts hanging around, looking like temptation. All young men were dangerous and desirous of good young ladies like his baby.

He'd come home sometime, tired, exhausted. Unable to take another step, from working so hard, from the loving companionship after. He dreaded walking in.

And his Talley would be gone.

But not this time, he sure hoped. Lord, not this one. He turned the key in the lock, let the door open easily.

There, at the table sound asleep. He hardened his heart before the relief could make his voice quiver. Hurried to the stove.

"Talley, you can't be trusted with nothing!"

Heard her leap up behind him. Books, sliding to the floor.

"Poppy! Din't hear you."

"Don't say 'din't.' How many times I tell you that?" he said, in a calmer voice. "Commere and get this stuff."

He knew how he must sound to her. There was just no time when he wasn't tired. Well, it would toughen her up.

She hadn't burned the chili. It was boiling, though, and runny. She could fix that with a little flour. Talley was wide-awake now.

"**Y**ou have to assume he does," Didi was saying. Talking about Talley's dad.

"I don't see why," Talley answered. "No reason to think that at all, I don't care what somebody talking about. It's not true." Meaning what everybody had been saying—her Poppy and a woman. A sweetheart.

"Talley, you have to assume it is true. Any man looking like he's alone prolly is not. He's got somebody somewhere. At least *one* somebody."

"Why!"

"Because," Didi said, "they do, that's all. Their gonads make them. Men are restless. Some woman always moving in on them."

"So why didn't he have somebody all this time then? Why come I only hear about it now!" Talley nearly shouted. They were standing outside the Colonel Glenn, ready to start the morning.

"He prolly always did have somebody. Maybe not the same person," Didi said. "Talley, you were younger and that's not what you were noticing. You noticing yourself together with your father. You never notice if he smell sweet, like he's been very near a woman? A woman wears perfume." She didn't wait for Talley to answer. She knew the answer by the stunned look on Talley's face. "Now you noticing yourself and *worrying* about what Poppy's thinking about you. You don't think he's human. You think he's *above* being human. You worrying about not having a boyfriend, too."

"I am not!"

"Oh, come on, you know you are," Didi said. "That's why you haven't seen what's right under your nose. You worrying if you get a boyfriend, is Poppy going to approve." She said it so quickly, Talley didn't have time to think about what she hadn't seen that was there under her nose. "You worrying who's looking and who isn't. You worrying about your body, what girl wouldn't?"

"You wouldn't," Talley spoke at last, resigned to feeling ugly. "You don't have to worry about nothing."

"Oh, girl, I worry just like anybody else." They were arguing now, like angry sisters, talking fast: "Don't you know everything is relative? I got straight blond hair, I want curly black hair. You got curly black hair, you want straight blond hair."

"Wouldn't I look stupid with blond hair!"

"Talley, you *know* what I mean."

"I don't want nobody's blond hair."

"Okay, but you know what I'm talking about. We always want what we don't got."

"I wouldn't have Roady if you paid me," Talley muttered.

"Well, thanks a lot," Didi said. She started up the steps. "Now you trying to hurt."

"Okay, I'm sorry," Talley said, and walked up beside her. "But I don't want to be blond!"

"Okay, dang, girl! You are really tough shit on me today."

"Stop cursing. Poppy says the Lord listens all the time."

"Oh, my God . . . I mean—okay, I'm sorry. So let's stop it. You don't be mean to me anymore, Talley. And I won't what-you-call-it, curse."

Talley sighed. "Okay," she said. She had to admit she was being mean. It was growing inside of her again, her jealousy of her friend. Turning rotten, like a peach with a patch of mold growing on it. Suspicion and jealousy.

But she'd got up this morning not remembering their anger of the night before. Didn't think about it until she was almost at school and saw Didi waiting for her.

Girl acted like she hadn't thought about the bus ride at all, like their quarreling never happened. Now they walked together down the hall as if they weren't even mad. That was usually the way it came down after they had their little fights. Talley was so glad.

"We missed you last night," Didi said, as they went toward their lockers. "Mama said she knew I did something to make you mad." She grinned wryly. "She always takes your side. Likes you better than me."

"You just saying that," Talley said.

"No I'm not. Swear, she'd trade me for you any day."

"How can you say that?" Talley said. She meant, it would sure hurt me if my Poppy liked some other young daughter better than me. Then she thought: She knows her mama loves her most, that's why come she can say that.

"I'm just telling you the truth," Didi said.

Talley had her mind elsewhere. She couldn't get over the way Didi looked the first thing in the morning.

Skin, like it just come off a born baby, it so clear and

smooth. I always got a pimple somewheres on my face. But she never ever get them, hardly.

All of a sudden, Didi looked serious. She was staring at Talley. "Girl! You don't even know!"

"Know what?" Talley asked.

"See what's right under your nose."

"What! You said that before," Talley said.

"Open your eyes, Talley. Take a good look around!" Didi said, like a warning.

"Where are you going, Didi?"

"Have to get to class," Didi called, for she had turned down another hallway. She looked back over her shoulder, giving Talley a backhand wave. Was that a fearful look? Talley wondered. "Girl, take care!" Didi called. She had shaped the words with her mouth. Talley understood her. What had been in Didi's look? Worry for her? Puzzled, she watched Didi go a moment and turned away to her own business. She had a study hall first period. She was lucky with that. She could go over her work for the day and finish the work she'd fallen asleep over last night. She had lied to Poppy about having finished it.

Poppy, she thought, has a woman. Everybody know it. She began a slow burn. It made her feel sick and tired all of a sudden. He won't even think enough of me to tell me. Won't even think I'm old enough to know, or to meet her. That was the way he was about the woman he never marry who was my mama. Wouldn't never talk to me about her. Someday, I'll find her. Ain't got the time right now. I know this new one's not my mama. Say she is half his age. He think I'm a baby young lady. Well, I'm not. I'm a grown young woman and I'll show him someday, too.

The fact that she knew for pretty sure that Poppy had

somebody would make her feel awkward around him. This morning, earlier, had been slightly different.

Guess I had to know something, even if it wasn't all conscious.

Poppy had gotten up as usual to fix her something before school.

"You want an egg?" he had asked. His face was drawn, his eyes unreadable in the dull daylight in the apartment.

"Poppy, I can make what I want, you don't have to make me anything."

He'd looked surprised. A silent agreement between them that he would make her breakfast. He was never home to make her dinner. That arrangement had worked as long as she'd been a kid.

Until today, she thought now. Suddenly, this morning, him fixing her stuff wasn't what she wanted. She wanted to make up for his being angry with her last night. But more, she wanted him to just leave her alone.

"I never know what I want to eat," she told him.

"Have an egg, it's good for you."

Too much cholesterol, she'd wanted to say. She'd almost said, "Didi says eggs have too much cholesterol," but she caught herself in time. She shook her head no.

Poppy liked her to eat what he thought she should have. "How about some toast, then, some cereal?" he had said. She agreed to that, just to have him finished with her and back in his bed. She let him see her eat some of the toast he fixed. She drank her juice with him standing there.

He asked her if everything was all right this morning.

She answered properly, "Everything is fine," and not, "Everythang fine," so he wouldn't have a reason to scold her.

"Get your work done?"

"Yes, before I fell asleep." She smiled shyly, admitting to the weakness of crapping out at the table. But she lied anyway. So what if she had?

That was all. He was still too groggy to ask her what work she'd been doing when she fell asleep over it. He would've had to listen to her long explanation. Sometimes, Talley even wanted to tell him her dreams, which she found amazing and he found so boring. All about flying. Sometimes, she said she flew to places like Iran and Egypt.

"I mean, Poppy, I wasn't in no plane," she'd tell him.

"Any. Any plane," he might answer and she'd ignore that and go on. Long dreams, making no sense.

"Poppy, I flew like an airplane over the ocean. My arms straight out from my shoulders. You know how kids become airplanes like that? I could see this whole town with a building getting bigger and bigger as I flew along the coast."

"You can't leave yet, young lady," he told her once. "Don't you even dream about leaving until you've had your schooling."

She hadn't been thinking about that at all, she'd told him. He figured she had. Round about the junior and senior years, the black kids wanted to grow up, leave the community. It made him sick. He thought of Rochella, who only wanted his happiness, and his insides churned for her.

He cleared his throat then, seeing Talley eat her breakfast. "Well," he said, "see you tonight, then. Call if you need anything. You have the number? You didn't lose it?"

"Yes, I have it," she said. "I'll be fine, Poppy. See you tonight."

They no longer kissed good-bye in the morning, although she still wanted to. She sensed that it made
Poppy uneasy when she got too close to him. He went
back to bed.

Empty. That's how she felt in the apartment. Empty,
inside the rooms, inside herself, where the dust lived.
She'd gone to school after pouring out half the cereal
and smashing it down the drain. But it wasn't until long
after her first-period study hall that she became aware.

After she'd seen Didi one more time and Didi had said,
"Girl, you better had open your eyes." Didi with Roady,
wrapped in each other's arms.

"A White Romance—hi," she said, before she thought,
glad to see them.

"You don't call us that, I told you!" Didi yelled at
Talley.

"What's a-matter with you, girl? Roady doesn't mind—
A White Romance?—you hear everybody saying it. And I
made it up," Talley said, proudly.

"When are you going to get it through your thick
head!" Didi said, angrily. "How many times I have to tell
you? You think I like what happened in front of everybody? I know what they think of me."

Didi looked furious. Talley hadn't known what to say.
She thought A White Romance was beautiful. She shook
her head at Didi. But just then, Roady felt real sick. He
hadn't looked good at all. Said he'd go on home, and he
did, before noon, it was.

Now Didi was fixing to get the cramps so she could go
see about him. The girls would use monthlies when they
absolutely had to get away.

"What was the matter with him?" Talley asked her.
"He looked dead white." He had looked worse than that.
Roady's skin was like paste streaked with some pink dye,

Talley had thought. "Looking like he was about to faint dead away."

She shut up when she saw Didi seemed about to cry. "Girl?"

"He does it too *much* now," Didi whispered, tearful. "He does it all the *time!*"

"What?" Talley said. "You mean . . . what's in the box? Pills and stuff?"

But Didi clamped her mouth shut. She went on her way, to get sick so she could leave school.

I don't want to think about any White Romance, nothing, Talley thought, worrying about Roady. Got to spend the rest of the day by myself!

But she had noticed something. Only, it didn't come together for her, until lunchtime. It didn't make sense to her until two periods into the afternoon and gym on the playing field. When she thought she would do some running across the playing fields before any organized, class soccer started up. Get Didi and Roady off her mind. She missed Didi. She did care about Roady—he was a sweet guy, never hurt a soul but himself.

The official teams usually played the students not on the teams in the gym period. The teams split up and helped out the girls not on teams who couldn't play so well.

Without Didi in school, the day was too long and Talley felt too alone. She rarely hung out with anyone else. The be-black girls left her alone. Oh, there was still The Neighborhood stuff, but they all were moody and jumpy now that they were old enough to think about the future. What would they do when school was over? It worried them. They all wanted to have a special guy. Wanted to know that they were righteous and pretty.

It wasn't that the girls didn't like her. But she felt self-conscious around them, knowing they felt the same. They weren't as free-talking around her as they once had been. They thought white folks were so very different from themselves. There weren't many kids willing to let go their group and strike out on their own. That's what you had to do when you mixed with the others. She was one of the few home girls who had become close with a be-white girl. Not that the home girls didn't talk to the others. They talked, played sports. Now kids even kidded one another, felt pretty easy, too, with one another. But wonder and envy were always close inside.

See how the be-whites dressed, see all the easy money they had! Drugs were everywhere, sniffing and smoking, everywhere. Who had that kind of extra bills in The Neighborhood? Only pushers and hoods. After school or a game, it was hard getting together when you lived so far apart. Rarely did they go into one another's neighborhoods or homes, except for the official visits, like for a soccer-team party, or after a sports banquet or international dinner with parents and teachers. They didn't talk about boys of the opposite race too intimately. Never anything beyond, "Where'd you and Danny go after the game?" Or, "Are you and Arnie going to see the new movie tonight?" Easy questions.

Talley was feeling alone and jumpy when it came to her what Didi had meant.

Right under my nose! Emory! David.

Every time she moved, he moved.

Chapter
TEN

She'd be going down the hall. He'd be two, three paces behind her. She'd stop at her locker. He'd be down the hall, looking at his notebook. Not far away from her, either, leaning against one of the lockers, as if trying to remember something he'd forgotten. But not so she would even consider that he was after her and not so anyone would notice.

Just there. At lunch, just in sight and casual, two tables away where he could see her face. And then, step by step, maybe slowly have it come to her mind that he was staying in sight for her. She hadn't thought anything at the time. She'd been eating by herself.

Didi gone. Roady gone. She stayed with her pose of—"Y'all better had just leave me alone today, too." The only person who dared come close to her, within three seats of her, was Victor Davis. She didn't feel like talking to him, no more than to be polite. There were two guys hanging with him. Football guys. The three of them were at one end of the lunch table. She was at the other end, a no-man's-land in between, now that some others had finished eating. The two guys talked to each other, eating their lunch. Victor leaned toward her, with one of his long arms draped over two seats.

"Cat got your tongue today," he said, by way of a cool opening.

Stupid-sounding. She smiled at him, barely. "Not into it today," she told him.

"'Cause your friends be out dancing today," he said.

"Roady's sick and Didi went to take care of him. That's all there is to that."

"Uh-huh," he said.

"Well, you think I'd lie? What are you, man, a spy for the principal?"

Victor held up his arms in surrender. "Talley, swear, I'm innocent." He smiled at her, full of fondness for her.

"Well, don't be questioning me," she said.

Maybe he was grinning silly because he was one happy dude. Victor never seemed to have a problem about anything. His muscles bulged under his shirt. There wasn't an ounce of fat anywhere on him. He was so lean, he didn't seem strong at first glance. But he was all in proportion. He saw the way she was looking at him. Before he got any ideas, she looked away.

"You not feeling good today, Talley," he said, softly.

"I feel fine. Don't be worrying about me. Worry about somebody needs it."

"Then what's the matter?"

Happy eyes. How come some people never seem to get moody? she wondered. "I don't feel like talking to anybody. I'm sorry, okay?" she murmured, staring down at her plate.

"You don't need to be sorry with me," he said, so gently, just for her.

She picked at her food. She didn't look at him or anybody. But staring at her lunch—there were whole beets, cream corn that was runny, and chicken and gravy over little biscuits—she suddenly knew what was going on around her. It came to her what Didi had meant for her to see.

Smash! Crash! Like a bolt out of the blue.

Thunder roar, she thought. She thought anything to keep herself from glancing over . . . at him.

He was right over there. David Emory. And the feeling for him was ready. Any moment now, it would bust open inside her. He had been *at* her all day, she realized. It was amazing she hadn't been aware. Crazy dumb, girl!

The spike blow-hair, himself.

Lordy-lord. Too blind to see, me. Too busy in my mind! But I remember seeing. You know it's true, girl.

He been right with me. I know it now. Was, wasn't he? What Didi was talking about. You know you want to believe it, too.

Dude at the door of Roady's . . . Seemed like days . . . on the bus. What did he call it—his horse? Flyin' Home. *"Anytime you want a riiide . . ."*

Ooooh! She stifled a grin. Victor was watching her closely.

But looking downward, forcing herself to eat, she could tell what *he* was doing.

David Emory had two containers, half-pints of milk. Two servings of dessert—pound-cake slices with yellow sweet stuff dribbled over them. The sweet stuff collected in creamy pools on the dessert plates. All he had on his tray. No real lunch, no chicken or runny corn.

He had his silver bookbag held between his ankles.

Why not have it next to him? she wondered, fleetingly.

Victor Davis was eating. The two dudes with him, eating. She was eating.

105

You can eat and not remember it, she was thinking. Food goes down and I don't know what it was. I know it's food but I don't remember it. Don't care what it tastes like. What time is it? What time is it? Is it getting late?

Nobody sat down next to David Emory. There were girls at the far end of the table. Some female dweebs. Too weird to know he was fine. But no good-looking girls came within two seats of him, either, and you'd think they would, Talley was thinking. No guys, either. David was the kind of dude other guys liked to hang with. A leader type. Some other blow-hairs did come over to the table a few times. Leaned over, slapped his palm a minute. They didn't stay.

David never looked up at them. Put his hand swiftly down by his book pack. Then just as quickly, lifted the hand up near his shoulder. A dude would lean over, say something, shake David's hand and cut on away.

Funny, Talley thought. He's just too cool. David. Girls walked by and he gave them the once-over. When they passed Talley's table, Victor and the other dudes did the same.

Make me sick, the way they look at girls, all of them. They don't care who they next to, they have to look at some more girls. I never will care about any guy!

She did care and it scared her, too. Maybe I'm making it all up. I mean, who's to say that Didi's got it right? I thought she didn't like the dude begin with. And who's to say I'm seeing right? Nobody cares about me.

Victor does. Victor, looking at her, peeved at her.

"What's on your mind, man?" she said, reasonably, like nothing was going on. She ate her beets, spearing them one at a time.

"I ain't said nothing," he said.

"Don't say 'ain't,'" she said.

"If you don't want me to, I won't," he said. Listening, the two other dudes laughed.

"Oh, yeah," one of them said.

"Oh, *yes!*" the other one corrected him.

"Y'all just shut up," Talley told them.

"You want us to, we will," the first one said.

"Stop picking on the sweet thang," the other one said.

Victor turned his head sharply around at them. They sat at attention, pretending fear. But they shut up. Nobody wanted Victor angry with him. You could play, but don't get him too mad.

What would happen? Talley wondered. Would he sock it to them because of me?

She glanced at Victor and quickly down again before he saw. He looked gross to her, suddenly, putting away his food. Guys like him ate so much that you usually saw them with double orders of everything. Victor had a side plate of chicken. A mountain of beets that he was putting away.

Who cares.

"Hey, Talley . . . Barbour?"

Oh-muh-god.

It was the blow-hair.

He came over to the table. He had left his tray on the other one, meaning, he didn't intend to stay.

Oh, my goodness.

She made herself look up. "Yeah?"

"Hi . . . my name's David." He reached out for her hand, forcing her to reach for his. She did so as if it was the worst thing she had to do. Shaking hands wasn't what most students did. Their fingertips touched.

The shocking heat of his lightning made her heartbeat roll.

Victor's hands laid down the fork, the knife. Palms flat

on the table now, on either side of the tray. Other two dudes had their hands poised on the table.

Fight? Over me! What's this? she thought. Victor wouldn't do . . .

David was polite, the perfect-gentleman guy, acknowledging Victor's position closest to her with a nod of his head.

"I was just wondering if you knew where Roady was. I need to find him for something. I seen that Didi was gone, too."

"Oh, yeah," she said. "Roady not feeling so hot, and Didi left to see maybe she could get him to the doctor."

"Oh . . ." David said. "Must be getting the flu, I bet."

"Must be," Talley managed. She had to look at him. Victor, watching her and then gazing serenely, deadly, at David blow-hair.

"It's going around," David said.

"Yeah, I guess it must be," Talley answered.

She saw spits of light in his eyes. *"Hi there, Roxanne,"* she heard him in her head. Don't you dare!

But he wasn't going anywhere with it. "Well, thanks, then," he said. He nodded at Victor and went back to his table.

He did that . . . why'd he do that! He did that to tell me he's watching . . . I don't believe it.

Lunchtime, over. Talley stayed at the table, as buzzers sounded, forcing Victor and his dudes to leave first.

"Take your tray?" he asked her. Standing there, looking at her. She couldn't watch David leave with Victor standing over her. Although at the door, she saw David pause, turn slightly toward her. Then, he went on out.

Man, this is a strain. Didi, why'd you pick today to run out on me? When the stone finest dude has to start something.

108

Realized Victor was still standing. So she nudged her tray toward him. "Take it, then," she said. Sullen, at him.

"What'd I do to you, today?" Victor said. Eyes, almost pleading.

"Don't," she said.

"I'm not doing nothing. Don't what?" he said.

"Don't make out we're together, why you taking my tray."

"I just wanted to take it for you," he said. "Wasn't nothing more to it than that."

"Well, take it. Take it, then," she said.

"You too hard on me," he said.

"Then don't try to make me do what I don't want to."

He took her tray. "See you later, then," he said.

"See you," she said, evenly. Not if I see you first. You can forget later, too. Man, don't push me.

She felt evil, jumpy.

Maybe she imagined the whole thing about David Emory. Shouldn't even be thinking about the dude. Who he, anyway? was her last thought as she left the cafeteria.

She didn't see too much the rest of the day. Thinking so hard, figuring things. Kids, jostling, loud noise, rolled over her like nothing at all. Things were getting interesting, was what was on her mind, as she prepared for afternoon classes. First, here's Victor. He around me so much lately, I didn't see the changes were happening.

So Victor likes me. Does he?

It was hard to believe that he might be interested in her like a *romance*. She wouldn't admit that the thought excited her. And then, David, too. Couldn't be happening! How did these things happen? Was this how they came on you? All a sudden, two dudes? You didn't *even* know you had feelings until they happened on you. Until some guy looked at you strong and you felt what the

109

look meant. The look went inside you, waiting for you to feel it. Is that how it was?

Late afternoon and she was on the playing field. She had on her sweats. They would play soccer against next fall's reserve first- and second-string girls' soccer teams. The boys' soccer teams were out on the field, as well. All the kids not good enough to make the teams, or who refused to join, like Talley, or weren't into any sports although they had to take gym class anyway, would have to play.

But first, Talley would jog around the track a few times, to loosen up. It was hard to run alone, without Didi. She might ask one of the other girls to run with her. But it was nice to go at her own pace.

She ran around a few laps. Loosened up. It wasn't warm out yet, although it was coming to be spring. Typical weather for this time of year, she was thinking. And when spring comes, what then? Will I bloom, calla lily?

She cut across the playing field to get back to the bleachers. They kept their duffels full of jackets, extra shoe spikes, Gatorade and candy, on the first stand of the bleachers.

Players everywhere, kicking around soccer balls, trapping and saving. Balls rolled toward her. "Talley!" somebody yelled, and she started up toward the balls, expertly kicking them back. Out in the crisp air, the sound of punting, kids all over the field, all one person, almost, was what she liked so much about school. She should play on the teams, but better not to. Not to think about it.

She walked across the field with her head down, hands deep in her pockets. And it happened again. He was there. This time, he was there next to her. Slipped his arm through hers. His chest pressed against the back of her head, his waist against her back.

Talley stopped dead in her tracks. Didn't dare look at him.

I mean, the whole place seeing us arm in arm!

"Keep walking," he said.

"David, stop."

"Keep *walking*," he told her again. "You want everybody to make something out of it? Throw them off if you smile at me and I act like I'm playing around . . ."

They began walking in step, long strides, ridiculous-looking for her short legs. She couldn't help grinning.

"Da-vid!" she giggled. Her natural exuberance bubbled out.

"See? Nobody's bothering about us," he said. "So what of it, anyhow? I can take you by the arm if I want to and if you let me. Nobody'll object but maybe Victor."

"Nobody owns me," she murmured.

"No?" he said, easily, his lips down by her ear. She had to lean away to keep him from brushing her. "Victor thinks he does," David said. "He wants everybody to think he does."

"I don't hang with any guy," she said, firmly. Didn't dare look at him. She knew how he looked. Too good to be true. If she looked, she would have to make more out of it than it could possibly be. She wouldn't be able to help it.

"Hang with me, Roxanne," he said.

"You got a line . . ." she laughed. All at once, he put his arm around her waist and spun her around on his hip. "Ooooh, hoooo!" she hollered. Everybody within earshot paused to see. "David Emory, stuh-ahp it!"

"David Em'ry, stop it!" echoed around the playing

111

field. Guys took it up in a high-voiced mimic: *"David Em'ry, 'top it."*

Emory laughed in a way she hadn't heard before. It wasn't a haw-hawing laugh like with some guys. His reminded her of the pleasant-smile and deep-voice look of the guy in the TV ad on a big sailboat in a Bermuda Triangle race. A blow-hair all-American type—liked-to-died-girl-when-I-saw-him-looking-at-me kind of dude. Only, David was younger than the one in the advertisement.

He set her on her feet and slid his arm carefully across her back; then, put it through her arm again.

"Keep walking," he said.

"I'm playing soccer, man," she said.

"So am I," he said. "Listen. Tonight. I'll come by for you."

"No!"

"Why not? Your old man works."

"No, don't!" she repeated. Not to The Neighborhood. No way, and all the biddies and the babies watching. Don't you dare come.

"All right. All right. Then you come over to Roady's. I'll get us some hamburgers and stuff. You'll have dinner with me, okay?"

She paused. "Maybe I will, and maybe I won't," she finally said, not knowing what else to say. Would he want her to split the tab? Didn't know what she was supposed to *do*. Oh, Didi!

"Go over after school," he said. "I've got a couple of things to do—won't take me an hour."

"Well, I don't like to be there when . . . when they're . . . first together," she said, meaning Roady Dean and Didi, in each other's arms.

112

"Just wait in the kitchen. They aren't going to notice you. Hear?"

"I hear you," she said, softly, looking down at her feet. She couldn't be expected to say no. What was wrong with dinner with him?

"So, yes?" he said. "And I'll bring the food. What do you want on your hamburgers?"

"Just one for me," she said, slowly. She hoped she didn't seem eager.

"You want everything on it?"

"Yeah, everything," she told him.

"Okay, everything but onion." He brushed her hair with his lips. Squeezed her arm, and let her go.

He was gone. She spun around once to see where he went. All the girls were everywhere. One girl with long hair in his path. David saw her, looked the girl over, but he didn't touch her. Didn't put his arm through hers.

"Man," Talley moaned. "I mean!"

Am I dreaming? You know it happened. "It really happened," she whispered. "Got to tell Didi!" He likes me. A boy likes me! Having dinner—oh, wow. Well, maybe I'll go. I didn't say I *would.* Oh, I have to get home after school and shower and change. No. It's just casual. But you can clean up right here in the locker room. What you have on today is fine, if you decide to go. Nothing extra, don't get upset. But my hair, after soccer. Borrow somebody's blow dryer.

The day went as if it got stuck in the tree branches lining the school bus driveway and couldn't tear itself away. Talley tried to pull it along faster but it seemed to almost stand still. This time, school wasn't going to break out. She agonized whether to meet David or not. She played soccer the rest of the gym period. She really was good as a guard and she could sweep as well. But today, she played average so the coach wouldn't get on her about playing for the team. She saw openings on the goal which she didn't take. Girls yelled at her. She just hummed to herself.

When the period was over, she was still humming, figuring. All of the other students, ranging together, going in, guys and girls. There was Victor, too, coming in. He veered close to her in front of her. He turned to look at her. She smiled, she was feeling good. "Hi, Victor," she said, softly.

"What?" he said. She guessed he pretended he couldn't hear her so he could wait for her and get closer to her.

Honestly, he was getting to be a pain. "I just said hi," she said.

"Hi, Talley," he said. "You doing anything after school?"

I mean, bold! Just because she thought to be friendly. "Yeah," she said, "Poppy's getting off and . . . we have to paint the kitchen." The lie came into her head that quickly.

"Maybe I'll come over, give you all a hand," he said.

She smiled sweetly. "Well, if you want."

"Okay!" he said. He grinned, looking beside himself with happiness.

So he comes over and so maybe nobody's there. Serves him right, she thought. Then, he'll know I don't like him and maybe he'll leave me alone. Well, I don't dislike him. But that's the way you have to treat some guys or they'll bother you to death.

It seemed to her Victor would be like an old worn shoe. Familiar. Something comfortable to wear when you were tired, aching all over.

114

Chapter
ELEVEN

ven with the kitchen door shut, Priest seeped in, filling the room with its frantic beat.

"You could turn it down a little," Talley managed over the music. The metal energy of Priest'd made their dinner together seem hurried.

"Oh. Uhnh." David's mouth was wrapped around one of three burgers he'd ordered for himself. Still chewing, he got up and went out to see about the music. After a moment the loudness of the Priest tape was lowered.

There, she thought. Nice, to have the music in the background now, so her attention wouldn't stray.

No chance of that, she thought. How'm I going to pay less attention with him looking at me the way he does? Those shoulders! David had the broadest shoulders, she thought. Wow. Here I am with him in here. I can't believe it.

She had come on over. First, she'd decided not to come; then, had talked herself into it. Told Didi over the phone to be sure to leave the door unlocked.

"Have to meet somebody over Roady's," she said. Then, listened closely to her friend.

"So he got to you," Didi said. "David Hollywood."

Talley ignored the dig. "Look, he only asked me to come have dinner with him over there. It's okay, isn't it," she asked, "if I decide to?" She acted as bold as she could about it.

"Sure, it's okay, but think twice, Talley," Didi'd said. Her voice had seemed strained, like she was holding back something.

Talley didn't have time to worry about it. She'd finally made up her mind to go over, feeling both fearful and excited by the idea.

Music blasting, as usual, as she went in. She'd turned her eyes away from them under the covers across the room and had gone straight to the kitchen. It wasn't twenty minutes before David came in with a bag full of food.

The way they looked at one another from the very first moment of being alone together. Made everything seem to go into slow motion. Seem right. Every detail about him—his hair, his hands, his nails, shoulders—passed in slo-mo to Talley's memory forever. He stood with his back against the closed door, staring at her. His look was so alert, like he would drench her in the light out of his eyes.

"Hey," he said, gazing all over her face and neck, then down.

"Hey, yourself," she'd said, casually. Heart beating hard against her chest. Neither one of them had smiled. Strange. But they were into each other, she could feel it. They were more together than just being in the kitchen having hamburgers alone for the first time. The pull was

116

strong between them. They were pulling each other in. She resisted the pull.

Now, David returned to the table. Priest was a manageable sound.

Do what you wanna do. Oh, what you put me though.
How I suffered for you.
Say what you want to say. Know what you gotta
pay . . .

He attacked his hamburgers again. "Okay? That low enough?" Stuffing his mouth. He did seem to love the Big Macs. "Any lower and Roady'd prob'ly take my head off."

"It's okay, it's low enough," she told him.

"Is your hamburger all right?"

"Yeah, it's fine," she said.

"Then why aren't you eating it?"

"I am eating it," she said.

"You are not. Why aren't you eating it? You don't like it? You want one of mine? You want me to get you something else? Some McNuggets?"

You got me tied up. Dog upon a leash.
Instead of messin' 'round, practice what you preach.
Your days are numbered. My day's arrived . . .

"It's fine, no kidding. How'm I going to eat with you talking so much?" She giggled at him.

You give me pain, but you bring me pleasure.
Get out of my life.

He picked up everything, including his chair, to move closer to her on her side of the table. "Too far away, couldn't see you good," he told her, his mouth full.

"Oh, right!" she said.

117

He froze with his mouth hanging open. The chewed food lay on his tongue and coated his teeth.

She yelled, "*David!* Oooh, that is so gross!"

Eyes wide and staring at her, frozen on her. He made himself look ugly, if that were possible. It was. "You are grossing me out. Close your mouth, yuk pudding!" She squealed with laughter. He wouldn't stop and it was funny after all.

Then, laughing, she nearly choked. Couldn't get her breath.

He slapped her on her back. He quit fooling around then. She came out of it and he patted her back. She felt his hand on her as she got control of herself again.

"Whew! Went down my windpipe." She cleared her throat, coughed a minute.

"That's the first time a woman's ever choked over me," he said.

She giggled again. But her, a woman!

"Anyway, I just had to get close enough to see how pretty you are," he said.

"Oh, sure," she said, delighted.

"I mean it." He chewed and swallowed. "I mean, gulp, you are some beautiful fox."

"Thanks! After grossing me out like that." Letting him know she didn't believe the jive. Not a word of it. But she sure loved hearing it.

"I'll have to get some of the 'prim' out of you, as in 'prim and proper,'" he said.

. . . Say what you wanta say
But you know that you're gonna pay . . .

They were close together. He had his hand on her back still, moving it up and down in a gentle massage. He

118

wasn't doing anything that she thought she needed to stop.

It's nothing. Just being friendly.

She felt so near him, and it was nice to feel that. No heat of him shot through her from his hand. Funny how one minute he could be electric. The next minute, his touch was nothing more than friendly.

He smiled at her, said, "Little Miss Prim and Proper Roxanne."

A put-down, that quick. "Don't call me that," she said. Her voice broke. She kept her eyes on her plate. Suddenly, she knew she would cry. She was just so nervous. God, that fast, her eyes filled with tears; she was full of emptiness. Lonely for—she wasn't sure what. Why was she so simple, acting like a baby!

"Hey," softly, he said. Putting his arm around her, he held her by the shoulder, squeezed her closer to him. "Hey." Lips in her hair.

Oh, God! He smelled like a guy, she never knew could smell so nice.

"Listen," he said. Lips on her ear now. Made chills down her spine. "It was a stupid joke. Don't cry. I won't ever call you that again—okay? I'm sorry. Hey, really, don't be so sensitive. Don't cry."

"I'm . . . not crying," she squeaked at him. Feeling so foolish. She sucked in her breath and wiped the tears away on her hand. She dried her fingers on her sweats.

"Yes, you are crying," he whispered in her ear. His lightning swept down her neck. She couldn't speak. A tear slid down her face.

"I'm a first-class jerk. A wuss," he said. He'd been holding a burger in one hand. Now, he dropped it on his plate. Suddenly, he socked himself in the jaw. Jolted

119

himself backwards. She didn't know whether the act was pretend or not. But he almost fell off the chair; she landed against him, nearly into his lap. She screamed, suddenly laughing, as he pulled her over on him and wrapped his arms around her.

I'd spend the days alone. I use to stay at home.
Lost in seclusion there.
Like I was in a cell. I kept your heart as well.
Surrounded by despair . . .

He buried his face in her neck. "Ummm," blowing air against her skin. "Sweeeet," he said. His heat went right through her. It made her giggle and squirm. Feelings shot around her stomach.

Fever! You set my soul on fire.
Fever! You fill me with desire.

"David, stop." She pulled away from him. Felt over-heated and awkward. She managed to sit up straight before she lost more control.

He was smiling at her. She chose to keep her face half turned away.

"You are a terror!" she told him. No more tears now.

Fever! You always get it right.
Fever! All day and all night . . .

"Least, I'm myself," he said. And then: "I like the way you smell."

His voice, so much a man's. The way I smell? She felt so shy with him. Didn't know how to act. And never knew what to say. His arm was still around her. She couldn't tell him to take it away. But she wanted him to; then, she didn't want him to.

Every time she looked up at him, he was looking at her.

"Eat your hamburger before it gets cold."

She took a bite. And didn't taste the meat when she swallowed it. She knew it was cold, though. She was looking at him and the feeling for him rose within her. His hand became fire on her shoulder, moving her.

She curved over her plate, shielding her eyes with her hand, her body with her arm.

He fluffed the back of her hair; held her curls away and kissed her neck.

"Don't," she said, squirming away. She felt like a dumb kid.

But at once, he stopped. "Don't tell me don't," he said, quietly.

He was for real, gazing at her as if she were a queen. She knew what might happen if she looked back too long. She forced her eyes away. She could feel his look boring into her. This time, she couldn't resist. Looked up at him.

"Haven't ever seen anybody like you before," she whispered. The kitchen was so quiet, her voice seemed loud to her. And it was true, he fascinated her.

One night as I walked, I heard your body talk.
I saw a shooting star . . .

His face came close to hers. She knew what he was going to do. He did. He leaned over, kissed her cheek. Kissed her chin and the other cheek, so gently. Her eyes, each eyelid. She never would have believed it.

"Don't," she managed. Her heart wasn't in it. She cleared her throat to make her voice sound better. "I wish you wouldn't." But he kept on after her. "Don't," she protested.

121

He stopped. His face seemed to glow with heat. "Don't tell me don't," he said again. The look he gave her was deeply cool. Light fading beneath cold, brown water.

She felt as if she were the Priest music she heard in her head, and he was playing her. "Listen," he said, "you think I'm some kid like that Vincent—what's his name? Victor. Like Victor?"

She stared at him questioningly. Didn't know what to say. "He's not my boyfriend," she said, finally.

"Yeah, but he'd like to be, wouldn't he?"

She shook her head, she didn't know that for sure.

"You want him to be your boyfriend?" he asked.

She shook her head. "I don't want any boyfriend," she said.

"Yes, you do." He grinned at her.

"No," she said. Their eyes were locked, faces so close. She felt him breathing her in.

"Yes. Me," he said. "I'm the one." And then, he kissed her on the lips. She thought he was going to. It was the softest, moist touch, so warm and sweet.

"Don't," came out automatically when he had finished, as she pushed against his chest.

All at once, he slammed his fist on the table so violently, she jumped back in her chair. "Don't-ever-tell-me-don't again!" he said.

There was a pause. She felt frightened, he looked so angry. Their eyes, still right on. She could feel them pulling her in, cool, sharp pools. *Don't!* Again, she resisted but she could feel his will. She leaned toward his darkening gaze.

He handled her with both hands now, pressing her shoulders. Up so close to her face, the after-shave he wore made her giddy. "What do you think this is?" he asked, kissing her temple.

She didn't know. What was going on? She felt like she couldn't get away from his eyes. She knew what guys were thinking about. Her Poppy told her all the time. But David seemed older. What would Poppy say? She couldn't tell for sure what was on David's mind. She couldn't believe . . . Poppy. *"Don't bring anything with light eyes in this house."*

"Look, you want to be with me, or what? I'm not playing games with you," he said. "Make up your mind, do you?" His arms, around her.

She searched his face. She couldn't shake her head no. Had she nodded yes? I guess so, maybe, she thought. But she never got the words out. It might be how she wanted it. To be with him. But not so fast. Am I getting your meaning? I like you, yes, she thought. And you like me? Wait a minute . . .

So destiny has brought us oh, so close together . . .

No more conversation between them. He was so fast. Everything happened so quickly. She wished the music would slow down. She never had a chance.

This is a dream. At last, I'll be with you forever . . .

Pushing the chair back, he was on his feet. And lifted her right out of her chair. She was up his body—where'd she seen something like that before? But this was different. He slid her down again but her feet still didn't touch the floor. She had to hold on to his shoulders to keep from falling. Looking up at him and he was all over her so tightly. Hard. She could feel him surrounding her. Now his mouth was on half her face. Open, he was swallowing her tongue. The feelings, like nothing she knew. Seconds passed; her eyes were closed. Her body had a mind of its own.

123

Drifting to music:

Hypnotize me, mesmerize me. Feel my willpower slip.
Lock my fire with cold desire. Loosen on my grip . . .

Her hips moved against him. The music didn't do that. He did. His arms wrapped tightly around her; his mouth melted to hers. Now she was heat to his fire. They went on and on, burning, blistering. For a long while. Until he stopped it. Looking at her with such passion, he swung her back and forth in his arms, then, let her go.

She felt as if she were on empty as she watched him. He was full of her.

I believe you're the devil!

He took a chair and put it under the knob of the closed kitchen door. Priest was loud again. "Pain and Pleasure," "Riding on the Wind," over and over.

David held her so tightly, this time she felt she would burst, splatter against him. Where had she seen some girl riding a guy like this? What do you think you are doing! What would Poppy say!

He turned off the light. David!

Kissing her all down her body, under her sweatshirt.

What am I wearing? What am I doing! Talley! Eyes, tight. Kissing was the deep of drowning.

School. Who, in the locker. That's where. Didi and Roady. How A White Romance. Is this it? Got started. No, this is . . . night. Black and white.

The thought of color washed over her in a white-and-black romance. Then, it seeped away. Until she couldn't keep her mind on anything other than him. They were so wonderful together. Feeling. Don't. Stop. What am I . . . ?

Going under, kill the thunder . . .

All that had never happened to her, that could happen to her, did.

I believe you're the devil's child . . .

All that she couldn't know before was shown to her. What Didi hadn't told her. She never knew she would be like this. Dangerous. Always had such control. Knew not to go with just anybody. Yes, it happens. You can resist, yes. But she knew she couldn't stop it when it was right on. Like Didi said.

All that jive—good young lady. Bad young men after innocence.

Poppy entered her mind, flitted in and out. He couldn't change it.

Chapter
TWELVE

In the dark there, her head on David's chest. She thought about Poppy. It made her shiver and sweat all at once.

"I have to get home," she said, out loud. The first words between them in a long while. She couldn't believe it still, that any of it had happened. She'd let it happen. It had happened.

"Don't go yet," he said. "It's not *even* nine-thirty yet."

"It's not?" Had she fallen asleep? Missed some of the time?

He laughed. "How long do you think it takes?" spoken in her ear.

She felt embarrassed. He cupped her head in his hand; held her face against his cheek.

"Want to . . . fix myself up . . . before I go." Her voice sounded little. Shaky. She hated speaking close to what they'd been doing.

He stroked her back. His fingers were cool on her skin. "You okay?"

126

"Um-hum," she whispered. Wasn't sure she was. All so many new feelings. Not all of them made her feel good.

"Hey," he said, smoothing her hair. "You're just like I thought you'd be. Didn't hurt you, did I? If I did, I didn't mean to."

Don't talk about it. She murmured, no. But she wasn't sure.

Like he thought she'd be. Was that good? What did guys think about girls who went with them to the end? And so fast! She was one now. "Oh, God," she said, despairing.

He heard and misunderstood. "Look, I wouldn't hurt you. I don't go around with girls without some passport."

She got his meaning. When the moment came, she hadn't had time to think about it. But now she knew. He had protection. She wouldn't get into trouble. Made herself believe that. Still, she must have been out of her mind.

Say in The Neighborhood good girls get in trouble. Poppy. Bad girls too smart. Oh, mercy. Glad the light's out.

Someone tried the door earlier, then went away. Probably Didi. Now she was back. "Hey, Roady wants something to drink."

"Please don't open it," Talley whispered.

"What's he want?" David called. "I can get it for him."

"Just some juice."

"Got it." He knew where everything was. Knew Roady's place. He got a glass and went to the refrig to pour juice by the little light inside.

Juice was about all that was in the refrig. Talley made herself small beneath his jacket, smelling the scent of leather. David was there in the dim light, his bare body looking to her as perfect as a god's. It thrilled her, made her squirm.

He handed Didi the glass through the partially opened door. He stood there in the opening in full view of her. Didn't he care that Didi might see him naked? Then, he shut the door again and put the chair back against it.

Talley got dressed. Took her sweats from beneath her, a cushion for her over the bare floor. David was dressing somewhere in the dark. And brought her running shoes and her socks.

"Thanks." Hate putting on sweaty socks.

"Anytime, sweets," he said.

She didn't like the way he called her "sweets." It was what he called girls. Was that who she was? Any girl? Anybody's. Oh, no. David? Do you like just me? Am I the only one? I have to be. I must be.

She was dressed. She got to her feet. You have to stay cool. They don't like you uncool. She'd heard that from other girls. But she was still nervous.

"Okay?" he said, taking her by the hand.

"Yeah," she said. "But I don't know where my bookbag is . . ."

"On the table," he said. "I'll turn on the light."

"No, please, I look a mess."

"Talley . . ." He led her across the room. Flicked on the light and she had to close her eyes a minute before she could see straight, find her stuff.

She had to look at him. He leaned against the door and pulled her to him.

"Don't."

"You have to stop saying that," he said.

She pulled back, but he held her. "Look at me," he said. She had to look at him. Her face grew hot. She

128

wanted to die. She saw what they'd done was still in his eyes.

"Talley, you're with me, now," he said. He kissed her and she went limp with her love.

Finally, he opened the door. She found she had her bookbag on her arm, her purse hanging out from a pocket. She had to go out into the main room.

Didi and Roady, neither of them was looking at her. She was surprised to see Roady up out of bed. He was dressed in sweatpants and a sweater. He sat in a chair, comfortable, reading some metal magazine. Didi was on the floor sitting cross-legged beside him, dressed, as well. Next to her was a half-empty carton of Kentucky Fried. Some soft-drink containers. Good. At least, Roady had something to eat for a change.

Didi turned slowly, gazing at Talley. She looked sad, dejected, as if she felt sorry for her.

"Hey, Roady, man," David said, "you looking all right from here." He flicked the volume down on the tape deck.

"Hey, man. What-up," Roady said, meaning, "What's happening?"

"I got four tickets," David said.

"Yeah? To Hay-lon?"

"No way, man! You know. To Priest. Priest is coming."

"Priest is coming?"

"Yeah, man, to Hara. In about three weeks. I got four tickets, man."

"Priest coming here?"

"I just said that."

"Are you serious?"

"Man, Roady, try to remember. I told you I'd get us some tickets. Gottum fairly cheap. Little exchange."

Roady turned excitedly to Didi. "Priest is coming!"

129

Talley went into the bathroom. As she closed the door, she saw David take his silver book pack over to Roady and open it. Roady looked at him and the bag with this silly, adoring expression.

The bathroom smelled sour. She couldn't find a towel to dry herself, so she took off her shirt to use it.

There was a towel but somebody had to have wiped the floor with it.

How can he live like this? Didi, with him. None of my business. Oh, Lord, I don't think I'm ready for this.

"Okay, later," David was saying as she came out.

"Cool, later," Roady said. He looked sane, if not completely sober. His skin was so pale and transparent. He didn't get up, although Didi did. David put his arm around Didi and around Talley, too, and walked them both to the door.

"Okay, ladies, I'll see you later," he said. Then: "No, just joking, folks!" He laughed.

Talley giggled, nervously. For a second or two, she thought he was going to make them leave while he stayed behind with Roady.

Suddenly, David hugged Didi to him. His arm was around her neck. His lips couldn't have been an inch from hers. Didi didn't make a move. He blew his breath gently over her face.

Talley saw it all. She went dead cold inside. She couldn't believe it, but she saw his tongue part Didi's mouth. He was kissing her. He wound his hand in Didi's blond blow-hair. Twisting it, pulling it hard enough to hurt her. Kissing her, like taking a long drink of a thirst-quencher.

Talley tried to break away, but his arm muscles flexed. They felt like hard knots. She couldn't turn her head.

Couldn't help from seeing. Didi, eyes closed. David watched Didi's face, kissing her.

It ended, but not before Talley's heart broke.

Why? Why?

Through it all, she'd seen Roady, thought she had. He was in her line of vision, almost. Him, reading some tour book, flipping through the concert pictures. He never once looked over. But he had to know what was going on.

David took one finger at a time out of Didi's hair and let her go. Didi stood there meekly. But she seemed shaken, looking down at her hands. Talley felt so hurt. She was furious. Ashamed at having to watch her guy kiss her best friend, and right in front of her. Why!

Like I'm nothing. Like Didi, neither one of us, is nothing much.

She could have cried. David shoved her out the door; then, held it open a moment. He stared back at Didi. She hadn't moved. He grinned at her. "Look at me," he said, so softly. Talley guessed she wasn't supposed to hear, but she did.

"See you tomorrow, sweets," he said to Didi. "Good night," said for her and Roady.

"'Night," Didi said, spoken with her head down. "Talley? See you tomorrow."

Talley turned her back.

David laughed. He closed the door, bounded down the stairs. She took the elevator. He was outside, waiting for her. He took her by the arm when she came out. "I was just playing around," he said. "Don't get uptight about it."

She kept quiet.

"Okay, I'm in the shit. You get mad over nothing. I'm with you, aren't I?"

He walked her over to a car—his car? She didn't know. She thought he took buses all the time the way she did.

"Mine and Roady's," he told her, reading her thoughts. "We share the expense."

You share Didi, too?

It was a big car, a T-bird, full size, still in good shape. She'd never seen Roady driving it, or Didi in it.

"Get in," he said.

Guys. Standing a couple of buildings down from Roady's. "Back in a minute," he told her.

She was in the car. Turning there in the dark, she saw David walk swiftly over to these be-white guys. Oh, don't let them come with us!

Metal, leather-looking dudes. You can't tell by looks, she thought. Yes, you can, if you know what you seeing.

David with these guys. She saw his silver pack gleam into view. Bodies blocked her seeing. Hands, in and out of their pockets, jackets.

David was back, driving her home. The silver pack was on the floor between his legs.

Chapter
THIRTEEN

Almost completely changed. She was home each evening before Poppy got home, like always. But now, she would be in bed, asleep. She let him think she had her homework done and was too exhausted to stay up. Leaving him his supper on the back of the stove or in the oven, until, later, he told her it wasn't necessary for her to do that anymore. Leaving a note: *"Poppy, I couldn't stay up. Thought I'd catch up on my sleep. Got some tests all the time now. See you in the morning. Love, T."*

He came home later and later now that she didn't stay up waiting for him. He never said a word about it and neither did she. She came home later, too, but he knew nothing about that. He could see she didn't need to talk to him the way she had when she was younger. His young lady was growing up. Well, she'd almost made it through the teens. She was going to be all right. He was relieved not to have to hold long talks with her late at night, or come home by midnight. He stayed longer at Rochella's. Had supper with her. That made his Chella happy.

Talley never said a word about the woman, that she knew anything. She did know. Kids would tell her. She'd got the whole story. Woman had a job. She liked her man and waited on him hand and foot. She had two boys, younger than Talley. She and Hale Barbour were tight.

Talley had her own thing to worry over. She was changed. She was chained. David. She had to study twice as hard just to keep up in her schoolwork. She never wanted to do it anymore. Never wanted to take the time with the composition assignments. Mrs. Evans told them to write about what they knew. That was a good one. She smirked to herself. Tears came to her eyes. She kept her head down in her government book in study hall. She couldn't seem to remember any of the chapters she had to study. Good thing she'd been keeping up all along. Because now her grades were going to fall. That made her feel bad. She didn't look around at anybody. She was afraid how they might look back at her. And all she wanted to do was to bury her face in her arms.

Wherever she was, he was. They talked casually now and then in school. But not much. He was usually near her, though, somewhere. That should've made her happy. It made her feel resigned that he was like an obsession with her. He enchanted and repelled her all at the same time. She couldn't get him out of her thoughts and her dreams, too. She didn't fly anymore, dreaming. And no matter how hard she might fight the feeling, he still fascinated her. She found him irresistible.

Talley realized that mostly, David liked controlling her. Being the one pulling her strings. He was usually in back of her or in front of her in the halls. He was by her locker before she got to it, making sure she came straight to it between classes. And he would move away as she came up to open the locker door. At lunch, he was at the same table now, at the far end. Unsuspecting students might be in the middle.

Victor Davis didn't often come near Talley these days. Whenever he saw David, he froze in his tracks, staring. David knew. Kept his composure. But something was building. Talley was resigned to whatever would come next.

It didn't matter that she and David weren't seen together. Everybody knew about them. Didi said so.

"They say Talley's got the one dude she shouldn't," Didi told her. "Say he's too fast for her and too wrong. And lots of hostile stuff that you don't want to know about."

It made Talley feel sick inside. "So what do I do about it?" she asked one day. They were in English, in the back.

"What you're doing, I guess," Didi said. "Long as people don't see you, they can't make up lies. And they can't steam up."

Talley had since settled with Didi about David kissing her that first night he and Talley had been together. She'd confronted Didi over at Didi's, up in her room. "Why did you let him do that? And you my best friend?" she said.

"You should be asking me why he did it," Didi had said, "and he'd just been with you."

"Tell me why."

"Talley, you already know."

"I don't know anything!"

"You do, face it."

"I don't know. Tell me. Tell me why he had to kiss you like that."

"You know why."

"I don't know. Tell me."

"I can't tell you. You know I can't."

"But why! Why did he have to kiss you?"

"It wasn't the kiss. It was a show of power."

"What's that supposed to mean?"

"Because I can't stop him. You know what it is."

"I don't know anything!"

"You won't face the truth, Talley. I tried to warn you about David. I knew you thought I was just being jealous."

"What's the truth?"

"You really want to know?"

"I really do."

"Then, think! I don't dare say it," Didi said. "He finds out I told you and Roady pays. You know what's going on. You're not dumb."

"Didi, I thought you were my friend—just say it."

"No. I am your friend. But I won't say it."

"Then you're not my friend."

"Talley, stop it."

"Then write it out for me."

"I can't *do* that. Maybe he goes, 'Didi, did you tell her?' and I go, 'No, I didn't tell her.' He goes, 'Well, did you write it down?' And I'd have to say I did and then, Roady gets it again. Hollywood's got that kind of power. So I can't. But you already know."

"I don't know nothing."

"You do."

Talley refused to think about it. She couldn't do anything about it so why think about it? Her goose was cooked. She was a dead, plucked ducky. Wasn't nothing she could do. She was in love. She loved him so. Love had taken hold of all of her. This was love? A night romance? Her calla lily, blooming in the dark. Tears filled her eyes all the time.

By the end of each day, David would tell her that they

would meet. They met where he lived. It was the tiniest place she'd seen. It didn't have a kitchen, either, like Roady's place did. It had a refrigerator with a stove on top of a counter in one corner of the room. Just about a third of a refrigerator, it seemed like. A couple of burners on the stove. The bed was a couch with throw pillows. There was a closet of nice clothes he had. No pictures anywhere. The smallest bathroom. David said the tub was a three-quarter one. It looked less than that. Here, they would talk casually about school, about a lot of things.

"Do you guys all live away from home all the time like this?" she had asked.

He laughed at her. "Listen, my dad and mom split, so why shouldn't I split?"

"That's all of you, just the three of you?"

"I have a sister, such as she is."

"She's older?"

"A year older," he said.

"She in college?"

"You ask a lot of questions."

"Sorry."

"She's in rehab."

"A rehabilitation center? For what?"

He didn't say. He looked out the window for a long moment, like he was searching the sky for something. Then he answered the phone. It had been ringing. Phone always rang. He said she was not to answer it and she didn't.

Talley was over at his place almost every night. Even when he told her what time, she often had to wait two, three hours for him. She didn't want to question him. He didn't like her to. She always waited to eat with him. Sometimes, he brought their dinner. If he didn't, she would fix something on the little stove. He liked that. "Little mama," he said.

In their love, he was good to her. Kind. But outside of it, he could be cold and silent. He would walk out of the house and she never knew when he'd be back. One evening, the phone had been ringing off the hook. David wasn't there, so it kept ringing. When it finally stopped, she had slept a little. Woke up when David stormed in, shouting at her, "Why didn't you answer the damn phone?"

"Because you told me *not* to answer it," she yelled back.

"What are you, a robot? I was calling to tell you I wasn't eating here tonight."

"How was I to know it was you? You told me not to answer it."

And he'd slammed out of the house again. That burned her up. One night she had to make her way home without him driving her over to The Neighborhood. She had to take a bus and she was scared waiting way out in nowhere. She knew if it kept up, something bad was going to happen to her.

What else more bad can happen? she thought. She truly almost despised herself now. She had a hard time keeping it together, and only Didi to talk to. Didi wasn't enough somehow. She wanted to confide in David but he wasn't that kind of guy.

Once in school, she'd been dragging down the hall and Victor passed her. He looked back at her and said, "You've lost weight." Then, he went on his way. Hadn't thought about him in a long time. She guessed she had lost weight. She needed more rest. Up half the night with David. So demanding of her. She hardly ran anymore. Didi got on her about it. "You'll go flabby," Didi said. But she just didn't have the strength to run. Didn't need Didi's company that much anymore.

One time, classes changed, lots of kids all around. Victor, right on her shoulder saying low and fast in her ear: "I haven't caught him yet. But I will. Just a matter of time. I've torn up three of those silver bags and ain't caught him with a thing. But you wait."

Then, David was there in front of her and Victor disappeared.

"Security's going to get a dog and then we'll find where it is," Victor told her, fast, another time. "He has to have it in school."

"You leave me alone!" she told Victor.

Victor kept on: "Tell the clown if you have to, but I'd like it to be a surprise. Talley, this is not any party-party. Everybody knows he deals. You hang with him, you'll get 'hanged' along with him."

"You leave me alone, I'll tell him!"

"I hope you do," Victor said.

No matter how hard she had tried to fight knowing, she knew David was dealing. It made her heartsick. It made her want to run away. But how could she run, live without him?

"Victor's trying to put you away," she told David. Long time, loving. She had her head on his chest. Him, clutching the back of her neck like it was a handle he had to keep in his grasp. She thought the best way was to tell him straight out. "Says, once Security gets a dog, he'll find out where you hide . . ."

David went very still. For a long time, it was like he wasn't breathing. But she could feel his heart through his chest.

"What else?" finally, he said.

"Just that he can't catch you with anything. But he

139

says he will. He says he knows you're dealing all the time."

"He knew you'd tell me, too."

"He wanted me to," she said. "Why do you go to school? You're too old for school," she said.

"I am too old, you're right. But I like school, believe it or not," he said. "I enjoy learning."

"And dealing," she said. I knew, I just didn't . . . "I would've never believed anybody like you could be . . ."

He pushed her away. "Let's go, sweets, time to go home."

It hurt her, the way he shoved her. "I'm sorry if I said something wrong," she murmured. She was close to tears. She couldn't stand having him mad at her.

"Listen," he said. He always would say "Listen" before he said something serious. "This is a junk world. People pop pills all the time. They even give pills to dogs and cats. Anytime you want a high, I know exactly what would be the best 'pop' for you to start with."

"I don't want anything. You can't make me." She was shaking. Fear was suddenly pounding in her ears. She had the worst, smothering fear of crack.

"I don't have to *make* you," he said. "If I wanted to turn you, I could. But I'm not into that. I *hate* that."

You won't ever turn me on, she was thinking.

"Listen, I keep Roady cool, or he'd be dead by now," David was saying. "He's an addictive personality. He and my sister used to be tight. She turned on all kinds of people. That's how she got her kicks. She really was the bad seed. I hate her guts. I got Roady away from her by giving him Didi."

"You *gave* . . ." Talley began. It was shocking. Didi, a gift. "But I thought . . ." She thought Roady had first seen Didi in the Magnet.

140

David was looking at her with that cold amusement he had sometimes. Cold light under water. Always, the look reminded her of that; made him seem a hundred years old.

"Well. However you want to say it. I was taking Didi out, so to speak." He laughed. So sure of himself. "He saw her and asked about her. Roady fell. He really was in good shape then. And Didi was very good-looking. Roady's in pretty good shape now. He's been worse."

You are sick. It made her sick, herself, to know that David was about as awful as there was. She didn't dare even think what Poppy would say. Never ever would she have thought she could adore such bad news.

"Listen," he said, "Roady needs his candy. He's not the only one. He's my buddy. Better that he get what he needs from a friend than from people who don't give a shit. I don't hurt anybody. They ought to pay me for keeping the school cool. The black dudes from The Neighborhood who deal are known, so they can't deal in school. Some other cats know me and know to keep out. So, long as I'm there, nobody deals much but me."

He grinned at her. "If you find out anybody else is dealing heavy, you know I'm hanged."

Someday, she thought, somebody'll stab you through the heart.

All at once, he grabbed her and swung her off her feet up in the air. He buried his face against her. So tight. So strong.

She closed her eyes. Gradually, she gave in, melted to his touch.

Long time, swinging her slowly back and forth against him. They were cheek to cheek, so close. "Talley, don't hate me." She'd never heard his voice like that. It came from somewhere way inside him, muffled and sad.

"I don't hate you. Sometimes I wish . . . things were different. But I could never hate you."

They fell back on the pillows.

"Don't leave me."

"Oh, David! There's just so much against us."

"I want you. Stay with me."

"Well, I'm not going anywhere."

"Victor will try to make you."

She was silent a long time, thinking. Victor. Her Poppy, too. At last, she said, "Nobody can make me do anything I don't want to do."

He held her tightly. Kissed her and loved her. She faded away inside the blackest, whitest romance. And then, he molded her into herself again, let her loose. He turned on his back and covered his eyes.

"David," she said, after a while, "you're going to get caught."

"Oh, please."

"Leave the silver bag home."

"The silver bag! The silver bag!" he mimicked, yelling at her. "You, stupid! Good! Good! Christ, I could turn on the principal. You think I couldn't?"

"David."

"Maybe he's already turned on. Screw it! The whole world is turned on. Because a guy wears a tie every day, people think he's Mr. Flat-out good-and-perfect. How do you think I get away with dealing? Because I'm white and good-looking and act like I have some manners. Hey, Hollywood! And don't fit the stereotype of black and bad."

"David . . ."

"Shut up about it, Talley!"

He sat up. She closed her eyes. "Get dressed," he said. "I've got to get some rest sometime."

Made her feel like nothing.

She got up without another word.

He took her home. "Remember, tomorrow," he said. Tomorrow was the concert. So much time had gone by. She really didn't want to go hear metal music. "Wear old jeans and a blouse that has a lock on it." He laughed. "Wear old shoes you don't care about. Because you're liable to lose them."

She didn't know if he was kidding or not. "Don't carry one of those silly pocketbooks. A lipstick, maybe, and a comb. Nothing else."

She wanted to ask did she have to go. He answered that for her. "I want you to go. I don't like going without some sweets."

She opened the door. "Talley, I'm teasing! For Chrissake!"

"Okay," she murmured.

"Listen, if I don't talk to you in school. We're leaving about two-thirty."

"Two-thirty? I thought it started . . ."

"Sweets, don't try to think, please. There are no reserved seats. You got to get there early if you want a seat. You girls can sit, but I think you better come down on the floor with us. It'll be cool. I'll explain how you act tomorrow."

"I know how to act," she muttered.

"No. You don't understand. I'll explain tomorrow. Get going, sweets."

He left her off two blocks away from home. He sat there until she was in the house and he saw the light go on. He told her he always did that. She believed he did. And yet, now that she thought about it, she didn't think he could see the light go on. She collapsed in bed. But not before setting her alarm for six-thirty. She had to study, try to.

143

Chapter
FOURTEEN

"**T**here's two types of people usually at a concert," David was saying. They were eating burgers in the car, in Hara's parking lot. It was three o'clock and they had to hurry. The line was forming. "People who are wasted are relatively harmless. They have eyes that are very small and red when they're not completely rolled up in the back of their heads."

Talley giggled, chewing.

"And they usually are getting sick, or they're sleeping or passed out and not very rowdy. Sometimes they're rowdy but not really dangerous because they are sluggish. They're kind of like sloths."

They were laughing and getting rowdy, themselves. They played air guitars and sang Priest songs. Talley hadn't felt so alive and free in a long time. David was so funny. He really wanted her to know what to expect, to enjoy the concert. She couldn't imagine what a metal concert was like. "You better had listen," he'd said earlier. "I mean it, baby-face. This is how to survive in the midst-a thousands of your freaking, metal natives."

144

The music was loud in the car. Every cool station was playing heavy rock in anticipation of the concert. David had cranked up the heat and the sound. He was driving, so he and Talley sat in the front, with Roady and Didi in the back. Didi had her head in Roady's lap, sleeping. That is, dozing in between near-silence from the radio when Talley got David to turn it lower so she could hear what he was saying, and the roaring metal music when Roady made him turn it up again. Roady was half-asleep, himself. There was a twelve-pack of beer on the floor of the back seat. She didn't know what all was in the trunk.

She'd had one beer already, herself. David made her have another to chill her out. It did make her feel more relaxed. It was freezing cold out. She had on long johns belonging to Didi.

"You got to wear them," Did had said. "This isn't no pretty-party concert. You leave your jacket, anything you want to keep, in the car. We have to stand on the line, who knows how long?"

"When do we stand in line?" Talley asked now. She had finished her fries and hamburger. There was more to eat but she'd had enough. David had bought her some coffee, too. She drank it now just to get warmer. He didn't mind cranking up the heat but it was car heat and it didn't quite warm her feet on the floor.

"Oh, the line!" David said. "Sweets wants to know about the line!"

"I'll go stand in it," Roady said, vaguely. He moved. Didi sat up.

"Roady, you sure you want to do that? I'll come with you."

"No, you stay here," David told her. "He can stand in line awhile. He's not feeling any pain. He won't feel the cold, either."

"I want to make sure he's cool," Didi said.

"Didi, you're going to freeze," Talley said. "We got the tickets, why come you have to stand in the line?"

"Oh, girl!" Didi said.

"Because, if we don't, we're not going to get down to where we can see anything," David told her. "We take turns standing in line until the doors open."

"When do they open?" she asked.

"Depends on how cold it gets or if things get too rough. Let's see, the concert starts about seven-thirty. They might open up at six-thirty."

"That's a long time from now!" she said. She could see that the line was growing, now about a fourth of the way across the acres of parking lot. So many cars were coming in. Vans, full of kids. Strange-looking, wild dudes. You could hear car stereos blasting clear through David's car windows.

Didi and Roady got out, carrying two beers apiece.

"Hey, you guys!" Talley said. "The cops see that, you'll get it."

They grinned at her. "Later!" Didi said; she kicked the door shut.

David was looking at Talley like she was stupid. "They're just rent-a-cops, your average Joes with security badges. I think they hire them just so the kids can verbally abuse them for about three hours." He grinned. "Keeps the nuts occupied long enough not to destroy one another. They throw empty beer bottles at the rent-a-cops and freak when the cops jump out the way of exploding glass."

"I don't believe it," Talley said.

"Then, watch," David said. It was true. Pretty soon, beer bottles were popping all over the place. The line looked like it was having a great time.

"The cops *never* bother the crowd," David was saying. "They don't know who or what might be on the line, so they don't mess with 'em. It's just a job to them."

"Lord," Talley said. She watched in awe as the line grew. There were metal dudes everywhere. Some die-hard head-bangers were first in line. They lay in their sleeping bags, trying to keep warm, or they were wasted, she couldn't tell.

"Have they really been there all night?" she asked David.

He nodded. "Some very crazy dudes," he said, "but they have the most enthusiasm. They really *love* Priest and loudness and rowdiness. They make it fun."

"You deal to them?" she said, softly. They were tight in the front seat, over to the right from the steering wheel. She lay in his arms, her face lifted to his so he could kiss her whenever he wanted.

"Don't be stupid," he said.

She was used to him saying that. He said "stupid" the way he said "listen" to her. It didn't mean much, she soon realized. He felt superior to her and most people. She supposed he was. When she was with him, she loved him a lot. But when she was alone in her house in The Neighborhood, she knew he was wrong. Knew that Poppy would despise him, not only because he dealt, but because he was be-white. She knew her Poppy was probably a racist in his heart, and that sure hurt her. Knew she was wrong, too, being with a guy like David.

She closed her eyes. "Why stupid?" she murmured.

"Let's change the subject."

"Okay," she said.

An hour later, Didi suddenly rushed inside the car, slamming the door. Bringing frigid air in with her. Her teeth chattered so, she couldn't speak. "Didi, girl, you

147

look awful," Talley said. Didi was shaking, slapping her arms and holding on to herself. She had nothing on her head but her long blow-hair. Her face was so cold it was pale rather than red.

"My ears . . . falling off."

"Commere," David said.

Didi leaned forward. David cupped his hands over her ears and rubbed them.

"Oh, your hands are warm," she said. "Ohhh, I am frozen!"

"Roady ready to come in?"

"No, but make him," she said. "He's all involved in some conversations but he might say something wrong."

"He won't say anything wrong. He'll just agree with anybody."

"Make him come in, anyway," Didi said.

David took his hands away and turned back around. "Got to go," he said. "My turn on the line."

"I'll go with you," Talley said, although she really hated leaving the warm car.

"You stay with Didi," he said.

"No!" she said. "Didi got to go with Roady."

"Talley," Didi said, "believe me, it's no fun. It can be dangerous and it is *cold.*"

"Stay here, Brownie," he said, smiling at her.

"Oh, it's because I'm brown," she said.

"No, not exactly. You're also female. But not too many brown folks like hardrock music. You are very minority here. And why wave a red flag, and a girl, in front of a bull?" He kissed her cheek, and turned up the collar of his leather jacket. He had the lining in it now. A warm fleece lining.

"So why am I going inside, then?" she said, feeling suddenly scared.

"In there, nobody's going to focus on you. They get swept up in the show," he said. "But out here, the rednecks'll be looking for amusement and I don't want them to single you out."

Then, he was gone. She did a slow burn about the whole scene. She watched him out of the window, trotting away. He was weaving around the cars and guys sick up against their own car fenders. Stupid guys, so wasted they didn't seem to know what they were doing. None of them were her kind, she thought, suddenly. What was she *doing* here?

"This is going to turn into a bust, I know it is," she said. She hoped it wouldn't. She had been having a good time. Everything was new and different and exciting. "Maybe I shouldn't've come!"

"Talley, it's nothing," Didi told her. "Everything's cool, inside. And we won't have to stand on the line for long."

"What? We still have to stand in line some more? I thought . . ."

"Well, eventually, we all have to leave our coats and get in line to get in. Maybe we have to be out there for thirty minutes."

"Thirty minutes!"

"But there are four of us, then, and it's like you and I are girlfriends, which we are. And . . . it's different, then."

"This is getting to sound like dumb stuff."

"It's just that it's the first time you've ever been here," Didi said.

Talley made no reply. She sat a long time, just looking. David had turned the motor off. Didi turned it back on so they could have heat. "He's got more than a half a tank. Let's burn it up!"

Not much later, Talley was warm again. She and Didi giggled and laughed together. She had stretched out on

149

the seat and her feet got warm under the heat. She sat up now, surprised to see how full the lot had become. "Wow," she said.

The line snaked three-fourths the way across the lot now. Sometimes, it surged forward, like a wave heading for shore. Then it would break and heave backwards again.

"It's like something alive," she said. "Amazing!"

Didi climbed over the seat with her beer to sit with her. "Well, it is alive," she said. "Those are your primed-for-metal American kids out there."

Trees surrounded the huge lot. That's where everybody went to the bathroom, including girls.

"Girls with a sheet!" Talley screeched. Girls spread a sheet between trees so they could have some privacy.

"Well, they got to hide theirselves," Didi said. "They got to go someplace." Guys came up, looked over the top of a sheet, paused, and went about their business.

"Ohh, Didi, what'll I do if I have to go to the bathroom?"

"Don't drink anything," Didi said. "When we go in, maybe you can make it to the bathroom. But I doubt it."

"Oh, Lord!" Talley whispered. "What am I going to do? What do you do, Didi?"

"Before we go in, we'll make it to the trees."

"Oh, no!"

"Listen, nobody cares."

"Guys with crutches are the rowdiest," David was saying. "They're always at the front of the line, too." It was true. There were so many rockers on crutches. They waved crutches above their heads, yelling, *"Priest! PRIEST!"* at the top of their lungs.

Talley didn't know whether they were hurt from war

150

or from accidents. But they were the ones who were the main cause of the line swaying back and forth. When the line surged, all Talley could think about was that concert down in Cincy when people got crushed to death. The line must've rushed the doors the way it was doing now, dangerously.

And now, there were hundreds upon hundreds of cars. The lot was full, lights were on. Thousands of kids were screaming and yelling. Laughing and moaning. They were sick with excitement.

"Why don't they open the doors! It's freezing out here!" Talley said. She felt a rush of excitement, herself. All tingling in her head. It was an enormous crowd. It's okay, it's fun! she thought. We're outside in the air.

"They'll open up soon," David said. "The crowd's almost big enough. "Les'see. The arena holds a legal seven thousand. They'll let in maybe thirteen thousand."

"Oh, my God," Talley said, and shook her head.

"You got any smoke, man?" a guy said to David.

"Sorry, man," David answered, not looking at the dude. Talley tried to make herself look small.

Then, two very big dudes came along the line stopping every now and then in front of the beer-drinkers. "You better pour it out or drink it. Now!" they told the beer line.

David, Didi and Roady gulped their beer and carefully set their empty bottles down on the ground. Talley had finished hers in the car.

She turned her head to see the two dudes. With a slight pressure of his hand on her shoulder, David warned her to chill.

"Not your ordinary concertgoers," he told her. "They're plainclothes."

"Really?" she said, awed. "How do you know?"

151

"It's my business to know. Plainclothes cops are all over the place."

"They looking like the other dudes," she said.

"You have to know what you're seeing," he said back.

Then, the same guy in front of them started a conversation with David and Roady about how much he'd seen of Priest. "I seen 'em down in Florida. I seen 'em in Texas. Ain't nowhere I ain't seen 'em." He was staring at Talley, bleary-eyed. He leaned closer to see better. "Hey . . ." he said.

She got a whiff of breath worse than foul.

"Yeah?" David said.

"Huh?" the dude said.

"Yeah, you seen Priest all over."

"Who tole you that?" the dude said. "It's true! You see 'em? I bet you ain't seen 'em much as I seen 'em."

"No, you right about that," David said.

"Hey, she . . ."

"I seen 'em only onct ba-fore," David said, matching the voice cadences and the accent of the dude.

The lined surged again from behind them and the dude fell on his butt.

"Man . . . why'd you push me? Who pushed me?"

"Ain't nobody push you, hog!" a guy on crutches said. "You wasted, man."

The guy sat there, blinking. "Is this—?" His eyes rolled up in his head. His face went white. He fell backward on the concrete.

"Yeah," his friend said, and began shouting, *"Priest!"*

They stepped over the fallen dude. He wasn't getting up. His pals dragged him out of the line, stuffed him in a sleeping bag and leaned him up against a wall of the arena. They had a short discussion. Then two more dudes on crutches limped with him, dragging the sleeping bag awkwardly between them, back to their car.

"I think I just saw about everything," Talley said.

"No," said David. "Look over there. There's a few examples of our low-life types, in from hiding out in the back hills of Kentucky. Extremely long blond hair below the shoulders, and hasn't been washed since they were in the seventh grade. There, babe, is your fruited-plains America, firsthand!"

Talley saw and nodded. The line was moving. That is, it was surging with regular frequency. Didi pointed out the girls. "I never can get over how you'll always see beautiful chicks with the most disgusting-looking guys," she said.

"Self not included," David teased her.

"Shut up, wuss!"

But it was true. Talley saw gorgeous girls hanging on to what appeared to be sheer scuz.

Minutes later, she and Didi made for the woods. "Last chance," Didi said, so they took it. When they got back, the doors were opening.

Not the time to remember Poppy, Talley thought, as he slipped into her mind. He seemed always to be near, ready to bother her. She forced him out again.

"Come on! Six-thirty," David said. "Time! Now, hold on to me," he told Talley, as the crush of kids began to move. "Please, don't get separated from me," he added. "You do, and you are gone, sweets."

The crowd swept them forward. It felt as if they were being sucked through the doors.

Like liquid up a straw.

Oh Lord, she thought. She had hold of David's arm and hand with both of hers. He had his other arm tightly

153

around her. But thank goodness they were going in. She was cold. Suddenly there were all these incredible, monster dudes.

"Hara 'bears,'" Didi said.

"This is the real security," David said. "Very large hulks who do not take any kind of shit. When they say move, you move. They won't touch you, sweets, but they will beat the shit out of me without hesitation."

"God," Talley said, "what kind of underbelly is this?"

"It ain't so bad," Roady said, sweetly. His eyes were shining at them. "My friends are with me and it ain't so bad."

"Aw, honey, that's sweet," Didi said.

Talley patted his shoulder. "Roady," she murmured. You had to love him, crazy boy.

The line was tight now and loud with screeching, *"Priest! PRIEST!"* Everybody, guys and girls, had to open their coats, if they had any, and pull out their shirttails at the door as Security looked them over. Some dudes were frisked. Everybody had to turn clear around.

"Anybody with some smarts can walk in with anything," David said in her ear. "Inside, you don't look straight at anybody. Keep your eyes in some neutral area. If a guy touches you, don't make a move. Don't curse him, don't push him. 'Cause if you do, I might have to fight him and I might get decked. They'll only bother you for a minute. Their span of attention ain't very long. Most the time, people leave you alone because they don't know what you might do, either. Stay in front of me if you can."

Oh, man, this is wild! she thought. Didi's not scared, look at her.

They were totally enclosed by rockers gone wild with happiness at seeing a live concert of their favorite rock stars. Didi smiled all around and bounced on her toes. The four of them were cold, but also eager to see the show.

Talley was ready for a *show*, as much of it as she'd been told about and could imagine. Looking around, wide-eyed, she'd never seen so many white kids in one place outside of a "the-slime-is-coming, run-for-your-life" panic scene in a horror flick.

This is a whole world, she was thinking. It's been going on, and now, I'm part of it. I mean, is it wrong when so many kids love it? Are they bad, for loving it? Then, I'm bad, too. Yeah, and a concert like this is something all ours. Grown-ups, Poppy, wouldn't understand. Not in a million years.

She saw dudes who had metal-studded earrings up their ears, who wore studded bracelets. They slipped the bracelets into pockets as they neared the Security at the doors. Gazing at them, she said to David, holding tightly to him, "There's enough leather here tonight to re-upholster every ratty couch in the state."

Chapter
FIFTEEN

There was a mad rush to the T-shirt stands, then a mad rush to "the floor." People were falling down. "David!"

"Shut up and hold on! You want a T-shirt, don't you? So you can say you were here?"

She wanted a T-shirt. Fifteen dollars? He bought it for her, fighting his way to the front, elbows out, her in front, because nobody was going to sock her out of the way, prolly wouldn't. As it was, she got an elbow in her cheek.

Got the T-shirt and forced it down over her head and clothes.

Didi and Roady had already gone down. Mad, mad rush. And noise, clamoring, kids, jammed tightly.

"Make up your mind, arms up or down," David shouted to her. They were at the floor, near the front and on the right side.

"What?" she hollered.

"Make your mind up." In a minute, she understood something that had always confused her. All those kids

156

you saw in videos of a rock concert with their arms straight up, pointed in unison, stabbing the air forward in unison toward the stage. There was absolutely no room to maneuver. If you came in with your arms down, you would have to keep them down, you couldn't move them. Same way with up.

"You want 'em down?" David said, behind her, trying to keep his elbows out.

"No!" He helped her bring her arms up. She realized then that she had no way to hold on to him. He must hold on to her. Too late. She was pressed against the back of a guy in front of her. She was a sardine. All of them were sardines. Nobody seemed to mind, it was cool. So chill out about it. Her breath came in short takes. The air was heating up just from bodies pressed together. It was foul air, from sweat and drink and stale breath. She hadn't even found the stage yet, she was so small. David!

The only decent thing about the next hour was that it went like lightning. She didn't have time to really panic. The crowd was still surging toward the front. Talley and David were swept forward and to the side. She was off her feet. David! She was screaming, but so was everyone else, which meant you couldn't hear anything but *"Priest! Priest!"* ringing the rafters like a giant litany. And something that sounded like *"Du Dah Es Priest! Du Dah Es Priest!"* over and over again.

"Oh, God!" she was sobbing. She couldn't turn her head to see David, to tell him he was cutting off the circulation in her arms, he held her shoulders so tightly. Somebody big was on her foot and that was why she was crying. She hadn't known. David!

Black Sabbath and AC/DC blared over the arena speakers. The crowd went crazy. The packed floor swayed back and forth and side to side in great waves of humanity at the whim of those pushing.

"Just move with it!" David hollered in her ear. "You can't fight it. It's okay. Don't panic!"

Don't panic. I can't breathe. I can't breathe.

People were pushing her, jockeying for position, trying to get further front and center.

"The opening band will be out any minute!" David said.

You mean, I got to take this for a warm-up band?

Somebody shot off a bottle rocket. The crowd roared. Three to four thousand people on the floor. Talley still couldn't breathe. I'm going to die, she thought. I can't see anything. David, help me.

"Can you see?" he called to her. She shook her head. "Well, wait a few minutes, and I'll take care of it. You'll climb up me."

What? She thought she hadn't heard right. She felt faint. I . . . I . . . She was going to be sick, and the concert hadn't even started.

Suddenly, the floor opened up in front of her. Just a wide opening, like Moses had parted the sea. She could see clear to the stage, they were that close. A fight had started in the opening. People had cleared quickly back away from it. She saw kicking, to the head of one hugely fat guy on the floor. Guys were kicking his head hard. He rolled over on his stomach. Two guys continued to kick his head. Nobody tried to help. The crowd seemed to enjoy the scene.

"You see that?" David hollered in her ear. "I mean, wild!" He sounded excited.

This isn't for me, she was thinking. Oh, I feel so awful. Oh, I know what's wrong. Like the time in the hall at school when she'd panicked with all of the students rushing around her. This was bigger and far worse. I can't take crowds. I . . . Something makes me scared. Don't panic. Don't panic! It hasn't even started. You got to get out. Out!

But the opening for the fight allowed her to take great gulps of foul air for a moment. Somebody had his hand on her hip. She didn't dare look to see when a face peered down into hers, grinning. Roady. "Roady!"

"Hi, Tal! Ain't this wild? I mean, wild! Ain't this something?"

All of a sudden, the arena went black and the noise stopped. People screamed. Talley saw flashlights bobbing on the stage. Moments later, stage lights came up, spots and colored lights. And there stood the warm-up band.

The guys who had been fighting quit it at once. The fat one on the floor got up and brushed himself off. Tally couldn't see a mark on him. He went about his business as if nothing had happened.

Maybe I didn't see it, she thought. Maybe I imagined it. The opening on the floor closed up tight, as if it had never been there.

Loud. Unspeakably loud. They were by the speakers. She could see them, three or four feet wide, piled up the side in great stacks. Noise came like a Mack truck running over her mind. Stuff began to slide in strings out of her mouth. She had to swallow it back. She had a terrible need to vomit, spit. She swallowed it and lost consciousness for a second. Her lungs felt like they would burst. For some reason, she had been holding her breath. She took elbow after elbow in her ribs. It wasn't violence, exactly, it was the crowd trying to get to the stage. She saw these guys. She wouldn't have known who they were. She was rising up.

"Help us," David hollered at her. "Climb up my knees!"
Somebody lifted her at the bottom. Roady. Didi was
there, lifting her by the waist. A string came out of her
mouth and settled on Didi's forehead. She watched it,
fascinated. Suddenly, it seemed, she was on David's
shoulders. He was gripping her above the knees. This
isn't me, she thought.

In a minute, Didi was on Roady's shoulders. And like
all the other girls riding guys' shoulders, Talley could see
all around. See clear over the stage. She could see the
noise strike her in the face. Lights. The crowd was break-
ers, was waves hitting, striking, up and back, up and
back. Shouting, screeching waves. Guys jumping all over
the stage. No, those weren't guys, that was the warm-up
band. Lights seemed to explode. Great puffs of something colored green.

The opening act was the bull's-eye. People threw beer
cans at them, showing their affection. The music throb-
bed and the crowd lifted their arms and pointed at the
stage in a rhythmic motion. Talley was seeing it all
through her personal nightmare of nausea, incredible
sickening noise, heat and mayhem. But how do they all
know the band is good? she thought through a veil in
her head, when no one could possibly hear them?

She felt as if her body had gone to sleep. Only her
brain was working, somewhat. She was swaying. There
was a surge and she was hanging to the right, then to the
left. Surfing! "Sit up!" David shouted at her. "Didi!" He
was shouting. She thought she heard "Take her out." But
nothing happened. She stayed more or less where she
was. She saw Didi shaking her head. She thought Didi
was trying to shake her head off. That made her laugh
and the vomit rose in her gorge. She put her hand over
her mouth as the ocean surged again.

The opening band did a throbbing set. The crowd stomped, whistled and roared its approval. Talley saw a fence, it looked like, below the stage. Bodies were pressed against it. A barrier. On the other side of the barrier between it and the stage was a kind of pit of security. The bouncers did nothing. They walked the line. They weren't there to help the crowd but to guard the acts onstage. They did nothing as people got plastered against the barrier. When somebody fell to the floor, they reached in to help. Otherwise, they kept their distance. We look like zoo animals to them, Talley thought. Monkeys and apes.

Behind her, she saw some guys in wheelchairs, still on the floor but at a safe distance. Close by them were a couple of bouncers who were there to see they didn't get hurt. She saw Motorhead and Saxon, Raven and Ratt tour shirts. Dyed green and purple hair, long in the back, short in front. Bandannas. She saw a guy close by looking around. It looked like something had eaten part of his face away. It was gross. She couldn't imagine what had happened to his face. She didn't know people could walk around with no face. Idiot! You don't walk on your *face.* She started laughing. She saw a T-shirt, said, "Randy Lives." Shirt with a guy's picture on it. Who was Randy? She didn't know. She saw a couple of black guys in the crowd. No black girls. Everybody was cool, though.

Somebody was yelling at David. "You wanna buy some weed?"

David looked him over, held on to Talley. "Give me a hit off yours!" The guy held his weed to David's mouth. David breathed deeply of the smoke.

Somebody else came up to them. Grabbed David's face in his hands. His nose was bleeding, the guy's was. "Did you just hit me?" he said in David's face. The crowd surged and the guy was moved way far off.

"Roady!" David said. Talley swayed. Her head was pounding. "I got to put her down!"

She was on the floor again. She had half-fallen down off David. "Don't!" she said. She was squeezed so hard, her face turned to the side against a guy's back. She was breathing like she had been running for miles. Drenched with sweat.

The crowd rocked. "Priest! Priest!" Lights went out. "Time!"

She was exhausted. Her legs, wobbly. She was being crushed. Her shoulders were numb. "I can't take it. David. I can't take it." He couldn't possibly hear her. She was crying again. Somebody ran his hand across her chest. She couldn't move. She was moving. She felt David moving with all his strength with her, further toward the side. Right side.

"There's a little more air over there," he shouted in her ear. "But, eventually, the crowd will take you where it wants, toward the center."

"Talley!" he shouted at her. "Open your eyes!"

"Huh?"

He had his arms around her waist and was lifting her through the press as best he could, using his elbows to batter his way. "Sick! Sick!" he yelled to those in front of him. A small space opened. "Vomit!"

But then, Priest was on, stage lights. She was almost stripped out of David's arms. Somebody slammed into her. It felt like her arms were being torn out of their sockets. Then she couldn't move, arms at her sides. David had one hand on her. She could feel it. Somebody grabbed her behind. Then, nothing. She was loose. *"David!"* Somebody had her around the waist again.

Priest was right on. Metal music. Familiar. She heard songs, love. Where was love? David!

"I'm here. I'm here. We're on the side now. You can see. Open your eyes. It's a little better here. Here, I'm going to lock you tight. I'm going to press my legs tight in around yours." Now she couldn't move. He had his arms tightly around her. "There, now try to enjoy the show!"

"PRIEST!" Roaring, surging crowd. Screeching, screaming, jumping, hurling metal dudes. Girls on shoulders, making bra offerings to the stage. Priest never knew if it was a B cup or a firecracker coming.

David was screaming his greeting: *"Fifteen years on the road, man! Fifteen years and you are still awesome, maaan! Priest! Priest!"*

Heavy rock steady. Groove. She was being swayed from side to side. Her mind moved in slo-mo. Was that Glen Tipton on the right? And K. K. Downing on the left. Lead guitars. And that Rob Halford at the mike. She knew them. She felt in slo-mo. Felt Priest move with David. Priest made her love the sound. They were good. She liked them. She liked the crowd now, as she was locked with David. Even though it was the crowd that stepped on her feet, got her with its elbows, smacked her in the chest.

Something exploded, and the concert came to a dead halt.

"Any more of that and we will walk off!" came from the stage, voice with an English accent. "We know you don't want to see any of us get hurt and we don't want to see any of you get hurt. But it's hard to play and dodge all

163

this shit coming our way. So let's cool it out and try to have a good time."

Then, it was rock and roll again. The crowd swayed and went back to enjoying the show, less junk thrown up on the stage.

It was a groove. "Groove," Talley said in her head. Her head was cracked, she felt. Ooze was seeping out of it. Ooze came down into her mouth. She let it drip out the sides. I'm sick. I can't breathe. You can't breathe, you die.

And she panicked. Thinking: How do the rest stand up and not get hurt? Not get sick?

She vomited. A wide circle opened up around her.

"Oh, shit!" David bending her over. He stripped off her tour shirt and wiped her mouth. He was moving her through the opening. "Vomit" echoed as she moved forward. People saw the shirt at her mouth. She parted the sea. Oh, look at that! she thought.

She was lifted. Dudes, big and strong, lifted her over. Barrier. Out of the zoo. She was passed from hand to hand. David met her on the other side. She was out of the area. They took her somewhere. Where she could be sick. David stayed with her. Bouncers, huge.

"I got people inside, still," David told them. She saw his fingers twitch. Was he carrying?

The bouncers were looking at her. Staring at her and David. She was shaking all over, violently. They gave her some ginger ale and a pan to vomit into.

She lay on a cot. Hand over her eyes. David was pacing. He leaned down to her. "You're okay now," he said, after what felt to her like three seconds. "Let's go. I'm missing Priest!"

All he cares about, Priest. Not me, she thought. After a moment, she managed to get up, shakily. She felt so awful.

"She's all right," David said to one dude.

The dude looked at her, said, "You okay now?" It was easier to nod than shake her head. She nodded. The bouncers went back to their posts. She didn't know where she was. But she could breathe. She sat there with her eyes closed, breathing.

"Come on, Talley, you can't be that bad off. Try to get control of yourself." David. He took her to a water fountain. There were people everywhere, but no huge crowd. They were out of the auditorium area of the ice-hockey arena, which was what Hara was, actually. She felt cooler air, fresher air. It was a gift that she would ever after cherish and respect.

Then, they were back inside, hit by a vibrating wall of sound. Him, pulling her close. She, holding on to his arm. He, leading her back into it. Why? Please! Not as close as before, but crushingly close. Metal music enormously loud close. She stood there, shaking and dying again. Until she had no more strings from her mouth and no more tears.

Until she was done. Cooked. This, someone. Not me.

Chapter

SIXTEEN

inter came down from the north like a
raging monster with wind, snow and sleet. The tem-
perature plunged and stayed down for days. Talley
caught her first bad cold. She was out of school for the
better part of a week and in bed most of the time. Poppy
made her vegetable soup with tasty slices of chicken in
it. He took care of her during the day before he went to
work and worried about her all night while he was away.
He offered to stay home with her but she insisted that
he'd best go on the job.

"All we need is for you to lose it," she told him. "Then
we'd sure be up the *crick*."

"That's not your worry, young lady," he told her. "See
if you can't get some of your catch-up work done. The
end of the semester's coming. You want to have the work
in. Anything you need typed, I can get it typed for you.
Just say the word. I know you don't feel much like sitting
up."

"I sure don't," she told him. She slept most of the time
while he was in the house, when she wasn't eating or

sleepily watching television. Poppy went to the drug-store for her, for cold medicine and nose drops, tissues. Neither of them thought about her seeing a doctor. Her fever never went over a hundred. "It's nothing," she told him. But she did feel punky. Couldn't get her strength up.

When Poppy went to work, she could relax. She slept more soundly then, until there would be a rap at the door. It would be Didi. She enjoyed having Didi come over, although it made her nervous to have her in the house. Poppy knew she came over. He had gone to work late one time, worried about his young lady, and had been at home when Didi arrived. Even now, the memory embarrassed Talley.

Poppy had stared at the white child at the door as if Didi were some evil spirit arrived on his doorstep. "Poppy, who is it?" she'd called, knowing who it was, knowing exactly how Poppy was staring, but fearing it might be David Emory, maybe even Roady. She had been fairly certain that Roady would never be able to find his way to her house in The Neighborhood. He might want to come see how she was doing, but Didi would have sense enough to keep him away. Never do to let Poppy get a good look at Roady's eyes, witness his silliness on occasion. But it had been Didi; Poppy had to let her in. She had Talley's assignments from school.

Didi came in. "Hi, there, Talley," she said, talking like a prissy-type blow-hair. Poppy watched her, to figure what kind of whitey she was. He had to admit, Talley knew he would have to, that Didi looked like the proper young lady who would be about good enough to associate with his young lady. Didi had made sure she was dressed right. She had on her winter coat, just in case she ran into Talley's dad, and angora gloves and hat, a skirt and sweater, boots and leg-warmers. She looked like a dancer, something. Like a movie star who danced and leapt across the screen. Poppy showed her grudging respect.

"Thank you for bringing Talley's homework. That is kind of you."

"No problem, Mr. Barbour," Didi said. "I can bring it and take it back. Talley and I are in almost all the same classes." She visited awhile, with Poppy just in the living room where he could hear everything they said.

After that, Didi came around four-thirty or five, when Poppy would be gone. She flopped in a chair next to Talley's bed; just sat there. "Damn, I'm beat," she said.

"How's old Roady?" Talley thought to ask.

"Still being Roady," Didi said. "Child is wild."

"You got that from me," Talley told her.

"I know it; it's true. He's doing better, though. I mean, he was awake all through the day almost every day this week."

"Good. How you doing, girl?" Talley asked her.

"Oh, man, I'll be glad when this semester's over. I am sick of this cold out. Roady's place is freezing most the time. David's gonna give us another place." Instantly, she looked sorry she'd mentioned David Emory.

Talley turned her face away. She filled up inside, with sadness and regret. David had called her twice since she'd been sick. Once, he had boldly come over with Didi, had lain down beside her on her bed. It upset Talley so, having him in the house and the possibility that Poppy might find out. They'd had a huge fight and David had left.

"Your old man's a clown," he'd told her. "Nothing but a janitor. You think I'm afraid of him? I'd be more scared of a sick puppy."

168

Even before she'd become ill, things had changed, continued to change between them.

"It all started with that rock concert," she told herself over and over again. "If I just hadn't gone to that concert."

After the concert, she had felt she couldn't go right home. David took them somewhere she'd never been before. To a countrylike place, a house surrounded by a fence. Two big dogs were by the fence. Talley had vague memories, she'd been so sick that night. But it was a house David owned. It had beautiful furniture, three bathrooms.

"Whose place is this?" she'd asked. "Who owns all this?" When they wouldn't answer her, she knew. They all had drinks and food. She had just ginger ale and pretzels. She'd had a terrible headache that wouldn't quit.

"Let me give you something, fix it up," David said.

She would've let him; but then, Didi signaled her behind his back. Shaking her head. "Don't take nothing from David," was what she was saying. Her lips moved. Talley read them.

"I'll be fine," she told him. "It's getting better." But it wasn't. After a while of looking around at his pretty house, she excused herself and went to the bathroom. The bathroom was as large as a good-sized bedroom with a black marble tub and sink. Quietly she vomited into the sink. Afterwards, she sank to the cool tile floor and sat awhile with her head between her knees. She smelled awful, like sour beer, like weed, a urinal, a sweat factory, she didn't know what all.

It had been a terrible night, but a night she'd found out about David all the way through. He owned Roady's building. Roady's dad paid rent to him. He owned the pretty house they went to. He had other places that Didi didn't know too much about. But once, she said, she was in this beautiful apartment he had out in othertown. People took care of his places for him. They cleaned, and such. Kept the places well-stocked with food and drink. David was into money. A lot of it.

After the concert, she and David saw less of one another. At first, it made her cry, the way he treated her. She'd call his place, the little apartment. She'd go over there, only to find no one home. She called on Didi and Roady for help but they couldn't do anything.

"He's just being like himself," Roady said. "That's David. Here today, gone tomorrow. Count on 'eem when you see 'eem."

Didi said nothing. But Talley could see in her face that she knew what was going to happen, as if she'd been through it, herself.

Talley saw David maybe three times a week and once on the weekend.

When they were together in the little apartment, he was the same with her. He might be loving. He could be cold. Always, he was completely sure of himself, wrapped up in his own insides somewhere. Sometimes he sat in a chair for an hour, smoking weed. He would sleep with his eyes half-open. She could pass her hand in front of his face and he wouldn't know it. She could drop pots and pans, he wouldn't hear a thing. When he smoked, his face seemed to melt, to sag. Then, he didn't look like anybody she knew. It scared her. She hated the sweet and cloying smell of weed. So she carried perfume with her to cleanse herself of the odor.

Didi came over that final Friday before Talley would go back to school, if she had no fever by Sunday, to bring

170

her the assignments for Monday. "They almost suspended David," she said.

"Oh, no!" Talley said. "I guess Victor nearly got him, then."

"Victor did get him," Didi said. "I mean, he found a way to stop him dealing in school. He took it up with the Student Council, no proof or anything. It worked for him that you weren't around, too. Security put the screws to David without you in the middle. Twice a day they dumped out his locker. They followed him in the john, too. Everybody staying a mile away from him. Then, the principal leaned on him. Said he was going after Roady Dean. David said not to; told him that he, David, kept Roady cool. So the deal came down: they'd leave Roady alone and David would 'cease all his activity in the school.'"

"They never could catch him," Talley said.

"Do you know where he keeps the stuff?" Didi asked.

"No," Talley lied. Well, she knew he didn't keep it in school. He distributed it late at night. People met him in the street or at his drops all over town. They'd pick up the stuff. He would allow trusted customers to pay him the next day. If they went to school, they paid in school. The bookbag was only his money bag. He knew they couldn't bust him just for carrying money. They might pick him up, take him to the Security office, but they couldn't actually hold him for anything. His lawyer warned the school about his civil liberties, about harassing him and other students, too. The word among the students was that you didn't mess with David Emory. He would burn you as soon as look at you was the further word. Had everybody believing it, too. But Talley didn't believe it. David was the best bluff artist she'd come

171

across. He took risks and knew enough jive and rap to keep everybody scared of him.

She also knew now that he'd been using her as a cover. She had a good reputation, once. Always confuse the opposition was his motto. Have Talley Barbour, be-black, be tight with him. Everybody would hold off, watch and wait, trying to figure out what was going on. He could keep up with his business longer.

"You need to get out from under him," Didi told her.

"That's a good one," Talley muttered.

She was back in school Monday, and she felt washed out but she was taking multivitamins. She'd go slow for the first few days. She bundled up good. She and Didi were in the gym, sitting up high on the folding bleachers.

Tears filled Talley's eyes.

"Oh, Talley, don't cry," Didi said. "He's not worth crying for."

"I'm . . . not crying," Talley said, sniffling. "Well, it hurts. Everything hurts. I hurt myself, mostly. I thought . . . I thought it would be . . ."

"Yeah, I know," Didi said. "You had this romantic idea. Well, what looks romantic is also real. What's good is also bad, Mommy always says. Every one side has another side, I guess."

"A night romance," Talley murmured. "Wasn't no good; wasn't nothing to it."

"Huh," Didi said. "Don't you go putting yourself down. David is just some kind of dude. I fell for him, too."

Talley lifted her head. She'd been sitting curved over herself, with her head on her knees.

"Same moves he put on you, he put on me, too," Didi continued. "He makes you feel you are the best thing that ever happened to him—for a little while. Then, you find out what it's all about, but too late."

172

"I still love him, though," Talley said.

"Well, someplace way inside I prolly do, too," Didi said.

"You do?"

"Yeah. Roady knows. Some soft spot for David, I can't help it. The first guy, like."

"He was? For you, too?"

"Yeah."

"Do you always love the first one?"

"I think you must always remember him," Didi said. "Prolly for the rest of your life."

Talley closed her eyes. "It's not over with us though, not yet. He still wants me."

"It's over, Talley, believe me."

Talley opened her eyes, stared hard at her friend. "Leave me alone, girl," she said. She got up and left the gym. She didn't need all the jive from Didi all of the time. What did she know? Talley was still seeing David. True, she'd been sick a week. But he'd called a couple of times. He was concerned about her, he'd said.

"I'm coming to school Monday," she'd told him.

"Good," he said.

"See you Monday night?" she'd asked.

"I'll let you know." Abruptly, he had hung up. David, who talked on the phone a lot, never liked talking very long. At least, not to her.

Victor was waiting for her at her locker in between classes. Just then, she saw David coming down the corridor. He saw her and Victor, must've thought they'd been talking. She smiled at him but he turned and went back the way he'd come.

She felt like chewing Victor out, but she didn't. "Move," she told him. She felt like crying. How you expect me to open my locker, clown, and you leaning against it? She would've said that, or even something mean like: Fool, stupid, dumb-bass, why don't you go somewhere? But all she could manage to say was "Move."

"Hi you doing, Talley?" he said. "Just wanted to say hello. Hope you're feeling better."

"If I wasn't, I wouldn't be here." She got her locker open, put some things in and slammed it closed again. She spun her combination, too.

"I guess you hate me," Victor said. He was looking down at her with the saddest expression. In a way, she was moved by it. But she was still upset about what he'd tried to do to David.

"I don't have much time to even think about you, Victor," she told him.

"He's real bad news, Talley."

"Just shut up about him. Why everybody think they have to mind my business?" she exclaimed.

"It's just that it will get around to your dad. I'd hate to see that happen," Victor said.

"Anyone tells my father is a *turd*," she said. Then, she smiled sweetly up at him. "You gone tell him? Say, Mr. Barbour, your little daughter been seeing a honky. Been going out with whitey. That's it, huh?"

"No," Victor said. "I'm not talking about his race. I don't care what color he is."

"You're lying. That's all you care about. That's all anybody care about in this place."

"That's not true, Talley. If he was black, I'd feel the same way about him. He's trouble, that's all. For you, for the whole school."

"You trying to tell me you like be-white the same as you like be-black?" she said, walking away from him. He followed her.

"I'm saying somebody's color isn't any problem. It's what you doing that makes it or breaks it."

"Leave me alone," she said.

"Talley, your dad's bound to find out."

She stopped and stood there, looking at him. He turned his face away from her. She had to smile. "So that's it," she said. "Victor, if you tell Poppy, I will never speak to you again as long as I live."

"Talley, Emory, he's just going to hurt you."

"But it's me he's hurting. It's my life. It's my life!" She hurried away.

When she finally did run into David, he was furious. "Tonight," he said. "Here's the key. You wait until I get there."

"All right," she said.

For two hours, she waited. When he came in, he was still angry. He flung things on his bureau. He flung his coat on the table. He threw his gloves in a corner, still glaring at her.

"You're mad at me for something," she said, trying to joke. She sat cross-legged on the bed. She had her coat draped over her, for the apartment was coolish. She wasn't afraid of David. But she was feeling jumpy, like she was alone in a dark hole someplace. She was inside herself, seeking safety.

"You like him? You getting to like the attention he always gives you, huh?" David said, all of a sudden.

About Victor. She shook her head.

"Don't lie to me. You like him."

"No."

"You like the attention!"

"Don't shout at me!"

"Shut up, girl! This is my house. And you are in my

175

house. And as long as you are in my house at your own free will, you belong to *me!*"

Always, she'd wanted him to say she belonged to him. But now, she was shocked to hear him say it the way he had. I belong to myself, she thought. But she couldn't say it. She just shook her head.

"Well," he said, getting up. "I've got to go out again. Come on, let's get this over with; then, I'll take you home."

"David . . ."

His face had a twisted smile. A long time, he stood there. His eyes seemed to glint at her. For a second, she thought he might cry. Then, his face changed, as though someone had taken a cloth to wash away all that was kind.

"Look, go out with him if you want to. I like you, Talley, but I ain't into just one person. I like to date around."

"Oh, David, don't . . ."

"Anyway, I don't think I'd like sharing you with some black dude." He laughed.

He came over, took her in his arms. Kissed her, loved her. But not before she covered her face with her hands, and bowed her head in shame.

Chapter
SEVENTEEN

"He really does care for you, Talley," Didi was saying. "It's not that he doesn't like you."

Talley was sitting on her bed, crying again. Didi was with her. Talley had just wanted to stay home, to be safe in The Neighborhood. Didi said she wouldn't mind coming home with her, staying for a half-hour or so. Talley was so miserable. Everybody in school could see she was. "You know what I think it is?" she said, when her tears subsided. "I think he'd rather get rid of me first before I get rid of him. He thinks maybe I like Victor—don't matter if he's wrong—so he's going to get rid of me before he loses."

"That's it," Didi said. "He can't stand rejection. And he'd even say something about Victor being black just to make it worse."

Talley had told her about David's racial slur. She sighed. "It's just that I like him so much." She put her head down on the pillow and sobbed like her heart would break.

"Talley, don't," Didi said.

"I can't help it. It hurts," Talley said.

"I know it does, Talley. But you know he's no good. Really, you're better off without him."

"I don't want to be without him!"

"That's the way it's going, though," Didi said.

"I know. I know it is."

She still went with David about twice a week, but never anymore on the weekends. Her weekends were filled with emptiness. Either she stayed home or she hung out at Roady's. Neither place made her feel very good.

When they were together, David treated her like a sick person, like somebody he had to help get well. He was kind to her, but as though he was making a special effort.

"Do you want me to fix you something, some soup?" he'd say.

"David, why can't you just be like you used to be? Why can't you just kick back, relax?"

"Talley, honey, come on, I'll take you home." Every time she questioned him that way, he would want to take her home. He got dressed again as quickly as he could. He wasn't hardly with her; he seemed always preoccupied.

In school, there was Victor.

"Everybody saying Victor's after you now," Didi told her.

"I don't care to hear what everybody saying. I go with David."

"Talley."

"Didi, shut up."

She wasn't ready to shut down her heart. Hard light of day hadn't broken over the night romance, not yet. Not for her.

"I'll get him back," she told Didi. "It's not like he's going anyplace else."

Didi didn't say anything.

Talley made herself more attractive. Once or twice a week, she wore a nice dress, with heels. She wore earrings and her belted Sunday coat.

"You look nice today, Talley," Victor said. "You look all grown up."

She had to laugh at him, he was so simple. What did he think, she was some little kid? He seemed definitely to be moving in on her. He followed her all day. He'd wait for her after class. She wanted to hurt him, to make him stay away.

Leaning next to her locker when she came up. Victor was wearing a beautiful new white, hand-woven sweater. Looking like some male model, too. But she didn't care.

"Man, you might as well quit," she said, talking softly. He leaned closer to hear. "I said, I ain't got the time of day. I sleep with someone else."

Saw his face tighten. Cruel, she was. His eyes ran away from looking at her.

"I know," he said, softly back.

"So? So, what?" she said. She opened her locker and slammed her books inside.

"So, I'm sorry," he said.

"So, sorry, what? Sorry whitey got there before you did?" Again, as cruel as she could be. She wondered why she was doing that to Victor, who never said an unkind word to her.

"No," he said. "I told you, I don't care about the color. I care who, that it wasn't me, I guess."

"Well, that's simple enough. That's clear."

"Yeah," he said. "I'm not complicated, how I feel about you."

"Never knew you felt anything at all about me," she said.

"You didn't give me too much of a chance to show you," he said.

"All you're wanting is what every guy wants—right?"

"Maybe that's part of it. But I want a lot more, for you and for me."

She didn't say anything. Something about the way he stood there, as if so much weight on them made his shoulders droop. She didn't like seeing that. "I don't know," she said.

"Talley, I can't stand to see you throw yourself away." Looking at her like he hurt inside as much as she did. Looking at her with all the caring in the world, with such respect.

"I don't know," she said again, "why you even like me in the first place."

"I just like you, Talley. Nothing else to it." A straight-out, uncomplicated grin spread across his face.

David Emory stayed out of her sight. No two ways about it, she thought. He's staying clear of me. Just like he wants Victor to take over for him.

It was a bitter pill to swallow, the way David was avoiding her. She hardly ever saw him now in the corridors. When she did and he saw her, he would pretend he'd forgotten something and go back the other way. Once in a while he would say to her, "Meet you at my place, five o'clock." He'd come up behind her and be by her before she realized he was talking to her.

"David," she'd call, not too loud, but he wouldn't stop. He pretended, almost, like he didn't know her. But five o'clock would come and she didn't have the strength to stay away. She would be there, waiting. Sometimes, she'd wait outside his door for an hour, tears in her eyes, ashamed, so ashamed of herself. He hadn't given her a key. Mortified when anybody came out of an apartment, seeing her waiting there.

When he did come home, he didn't seem too happy to see her. But he would let her in. They wouldn't have much to say to one another. Never any pretense now about what he wanted her there for.

You make me feel like nothing, she thought, over and over, when she was with him. Then, he would do something—smooth her hair all around, grip her neck in a certain way he had, or hold her tightly to him, and it would seem like they were together again, seem like old times. These were rare occasions, fewer and fewer good times.

"He manipulates people," Didi was saying. "David put me and Roady together. He thinks he's going to put you and Victor together."

Talley said, "I'm not a puzzle piece to be put someplace."

"But he'll try to do it," Didi said.

The three of them were over at Roady's. Rather than trying to find them a temporary place to live, David had given Roady a space heater, the kind that was easy to pick up and move to any area of the house. Now, they had placed it over by the bed. Didi and Talley were sitting on the bed, while Roady sat in his chair across from them. All three of them were feeling warm and cozy. Nice sound of warm air blowing. Talley had a glass of wine. Theirs was like a celebration. Roady had imported beer and Didi had wine, too. The three of them, the way they had been for so long—close friends, talking. Iron

181

Maiden played at a manageable level over the sound system.

Roady said he was glad Talley was back and not sick anymore. "Didn't like not seeing you," he said.

"Roady, I never knew you *even* noticed me much," Talley said. He looked like a hurt rabbit. "Roady, man, I'm sorry. I didn't mean to be mean . . ."

"Well, I . . . wasn't here a lot, I guess," he said. "But now I guess I'm back more. I always knew when you were here, though."

There was silence a long moment before Talley said, "I don't think I understand what's happening. I don't understand why David stopped liking me. He liked me so much, once. Didi?"

"What, babe?"

"What'd I do wrong?" She began to cry. Wine spilled over her fingers. Didi took the glass out of her hands. Talley rolled over on her stomach and bawled like a baby.

"Talley, don't cry over him, please? You didn't do anything," Didi said.

"Talley? Talley?" Roady got on his knees by the bed. He put his head next to Talley's. "Don't cry, Talley, oh, don't cry. Don't cry."

"Roady, it's okay," Didi told him, soothingly.

"But she's crying. Didi, she's crying. Did we make her cry? Don't cry, Talley. Oh. Don't cry!"

Roady's shoulders shook. He commenced to sob. He clutched Talley's arms, cried into her hair.

"Roady, honey!" Didi exclaimed. Before she knew it, she was sobbing, she couldn't help herself. The three of them were so close. Suddenly, everything was too sad. Too much to bear for all of them in this largely empty space. They were like children huddled in a corner.

There was something about the heater blowing, the winter outside surrounding them, that trapped them and frightened them. Didi held on to Roady and Talley.

Roady lifted his face, streaked with tears. "You know, we're all we got," he said. "We, just us, that's all. Didi? Ain't that right?"

He looked so frightened. Talley was frightened, too. She took hold of his arm and held on. She was shaking. Didi was sobbing so, she couldn't answer. And it was really all so sad. Just the three of them. It was as if they were the only ones in the world who understood everything about themselves.

A fine romance *they* were! Talley thought, her mouth twisting in a weak smile.

They stayed together that way, holding on, until the sobbing slowly came to an end. They were exhausted. For a long time, nobody moved.

"Huh-uhm . . ." Across the room, somebody cleared their throat.

David! Talley thought.

"I should've knocked, but the door was open. Sorry . . . I . . ."

The three of them had frozen at the sound of the voice. Now they moved. Roady sat up straight, sitting on the floor. Instantly, Didi stood and crossed the room. Going for a box of tissues. "It's okay," she said, huskily. She took tissues to wipe her face. She blew her nose, sniffing.

"I could come back . . ."

"No, it's okay," Didi said. "We just figured out how lonely we feel, sometimes. See, we all three come from . . . broken homes, I guess you could call it." She laughed lightly. "That don't mean nothing, does it?" she added.

Talley sat up. Didi brought her some tissues. Some for

Roady. Talley stared across the room. Her look said it all. What are *you* doing here? Victor.

"Uh, David isn't here," Didi said.

"I wasn't looking for him," Victor said.

"Did he send you here? He told you to come here?" Talley asked.

"No. Nobody told me to come here, or nothing," he said. "I . . . I was looking for you."

Talley stared at him. "You were looking for me . . . way over here. How come? You never came looking before." She didn't believe a word of it. He was after David. Or else, David had sent him, telling him, "Take her, she's yours!" Victor, she thought, looking like a cardboard cut-out of your movin'-on-up black male executive. Huh.

"Well . . . I . . ." Victor began, "I got this . . . anxiety attack over you. I thought maybe something . . ." He started over. "I was out-of-my-mind worried about you." He spread his hands in front of him, shook his head. "I just . . . wanted to see you in the worse way." Blurting it out, embarrassed. "That's it, Talley."

And all at once, she believed him. So did Didi, Talley could tell by her expression. Didi was gazing at Victor, curious about him and accepting of what he seemed to present of himself. A nice guy. Maybe a little too straight.

"You want some wine?" Didi asked him.

"I'll take a beer," he said.

"Okay!" Roady said.

"Hey, man," Victor said, "this is your place."

"You never been here before?" Roady said.

Victor shook his head. Roady got up and fell down on the floor. He got up again before Didi could rush over to help him. She looked stricken, her hand up to her mouth, fearing he'd hurt himself.

"I'm not high. I'm not high!" Roady shouted to Victor.

He rubbed his knee. "See, man, my legs is all screwed up. My coordination, buh-cause I been a druggie. I admit it. That's the first step. I talked to David about it. I've known him a long time. He said I was right to want to cut down. Slowly, so's I can straighten out. I been strung out too long and he agreed with me. You have to come to understand that yourself. Nobody can't tell you.

"See," Roady said, "I can stand all right, once I do it slow. I remember, most the time. In school, I don't hurry, I take my time. And I do all right."

It was the most Talley had ever heard him say at one time.

"I see, man," Victor was saying. "You doing all right. That's a good thing."

"I could do myself some real damage. David knows the signs."

"He does, does he?" Victor said.

"Believe it or not, David cares about Roady," Didi said.

"Maybe so," Victor said. He crossed the room. Carefully, he sat down beside Talley, giving her time to tell him not to if she wanted. "Hi," he said to her.

She didn't answer. Roady brought him his beer. "Thanks," Victor said. And then: "Talley . . ."

"What do you want, Victor?" she said. "I know you must want something."

"Don't be mad at me," he said. "You want me to leave? You say so, and I'll leave. I only wanted to make sure you are all right."

"Well, I'm not," she said. Tears filled her eyes again. "I wish everybody would just leave me alone."

"So you want me to go, then?" he asked. Something sounding so sweet in his voice.

"Nooo," she said, amazed at herself.

"No?"

185

She shook her head.

He reached out for her hand but she cringed, slightly, and he pulled back.

"Don't touch me," she told him. "I don't want anybody touching me without me telling them."

"Okay," he said. He took a sip of beer, then set it down.

She sucked in her breath, holding back tears. "I don't want anybody telling me what to do or not to do!"

"Okay," he said, softly.

"I just want to die!" she said.

"Talley, don't say that. You don't mean that," Victor said.

"You don't tell me what to say! I do mean it. I want to die—Victor, you never thought of killing yourself?"

"No," he said.

"Never?" Didi said.

"You never once did?" Roady asked him.

"No," Victor said. He looked at the three of them with such sympathy, Talley thought. "All of us come such a long way to give it up now," he said.

Spoken so seriously, it made Talley laugh. "He's into his be-black history and stuff," she explained. "Believing in all that uplift and do-right, and long struggles and shit." She didn't care how it sounded, she just wanted to strike at him.

"That's right. That's it," he said.

"You have to know his family," Talley said, sarcastically. "His mama wears a hat to the supermarket! And wears a dress and proper stockings and little high-heel boots all winter long. Woman wouldn't never wear a pair of slacks, now would she?"

"That's right," Victor said. "That's the way she is. We're not rich or anything. But my mother believes in looking nice all the time."

186

"Because," Talley said, "black folks got to look better, be better, work harder, stand up straighter . . . and shit—"

"That's right," he said, again, "just to stay in about the same place."

"Then why do it?" Talley yelled at him. "And they don't *even* stay in the same place. If they did, everybody wouldn't all the time be the last in every damn line, the last for every anything."

"That's right, too," Victor said.

"So I'm tired of being poor and living in a shitty place all the time."

"So am I," he said.

"So why don't you quit it?" she said.

He looked at her tenderly, so sadly. "You like him that much? You still want him that much?"

She couldn't say anything. Nowhere to hide her face but in her two hands. He was right on. She wanted to die because David didn't want her. It had nothing to do with being poor, or anything.

Victor sighed, eyes downcast and his hands deep in his pockets. "Would you like to go to a movie or something . . . with me?"

Suddenly, Didi giggled, then, "Sorry," she said. "It just sounded funny. I mean, talking about struggle—strife and all . . ."

Talley said, "She means, you just sound so *straight*."

He shrugged, looking mournfully at the floor.

"I know. I know what you mean." Roady, quietly talking to Victor. "You mean—somebody can screw up, like I did. A person can die. Your old man hates you. You mean, your mama misses you. You live by yourself. You feel sick." Words, tumbling out of him. "Nobody wants you. Somebody dies. You love Didi. Talley comes over.

You screw up in school. You a twitch, a druggie. You could die. But don't. Don't give up! You keep on going. You never say quit."

"Man, Roady, right," Victor said. "Right." He glanced forlornly at Talley. He shrugged. He wasn't going to ask her again.

"This is a school night," she said, after a moment.

"It doesn't have to be tonight," he said. "Just thought that sometime, you maybe might want to go out."

"Do you ever get rowdy?" she asked.

He grinned. "You think I'm a preacher, something?"

"Well, you're so serious," she said.

"He's on the National Honor Society," Didi said.

"That ain't nothing to be ashamed of," Roady said. Didi laughed.

Talley didn't want them laughing at him. "Thanks for asking me," she mumbled. "Maybe Saturday, I'll feel like seeing something."

"Whatever you'd like to see is all right with me."

"Yeah? I like that!" she said.

He shrugged, looking pleased. He got to his feet. "Well," he said, standing there.

"You come by bus? You going back to The Neighborhood now?"

"Yeah," he said.

Talley got up smoothly from the bed. "Wait a minute," she said. She prepared to leave. Went to the bathroom, fixed herself up. She put on her hat and scarf. She had already dropped her bookbag home. All she had to carry was her wallet. When she came out, everybody was in their same places. Didi and Roady quietly watched Victor, curious about him.

"Got to go, dudes," she told them, lightly. She went over to Roady and gave him a hug, touched his forehead with hers. "I love you, child," she said, in a rush of feeling for him. Nearly made her cry.

"Talley. Talley," he said, hugging her back. "Take care, Talley."

She went to Didi, took her by the shoulder. Didi did the same, took Talley by the shoulder. They stood there facing so close. Feeling for each other. "Girl," Talley said, speaking only loud enough for Didi.

"Girl, yourself," Didi murmured. She smiled wanly.

"You are beautiful, girl," Talley said, softly.

"So they tell me," Didi said, easily, uncaring.

"You know what?" Talley said.

"What?"

"I know why you don't like me calling you A White Romance."

"Let's forget it," Didi said, turning red before Talley's eyes.

"Wait," Talley said. "You have a right to be who you want to be. And I want you to know, you and Roady, are better than any white, black, or green romance, you hear?"

Tears filled Didi's eyes. She nodded.

"You are the *good guys!*" Talley laughed, as they nodded at each other.

"We all are the good guys," Didi murmured.

"Yay for the good guys!" Talley said.

Somewhere behind them, Victor was waiting. They both realized that at about the same time.

"Well," Talley said. She let go of Didi. Didi gave her a cuff on the shoulder, smiled.

Didi's eyes were wet as she walked them to the door. "Call you tonight," she said.

"Right," Talley said. "Tell your mama I said hi. Haven't seen her in a while."

"You can come on over if you want," Didi said.

189

"Thanks. But I think I'll just stay on close to home," Talley said. "Get up later, maybe catch up on some things. Come on, may-an," she said, to Victor.

"Thanks for the beer," Victor said. He gave Roady a wave.

Roady waved tiredly back.

"See you all tomorrow," Didi said, and closed the door.

Outside, the two of them didn't have much to say right away. Talley was nervous, and she could tell he was nervous. It was like they both were in a play, she thought, and they hadn't learned their lines yet.

When she walked faster, he walked faster. When she slowed down, he did the same. He wasn't so much watching her moves as he was feeling what she was feeling.

"You know something?" she said.

"What?"

"Does it feel—it's getting warmer out here!"

"Yeah, feels like it is, a little," he said. "There's not hardly any snow on the ground these days."

"It's getting there," she said. "Hey, you know what?"

"What?" he said, easily.

"Do you like to run?"

He looked at her. "Have to run all the time, playing sports."

"No, I mean, I feel like running again," she said.

He looked at her sneakers and then down at his own. "How about running to the bus stop?" he said.

"Yeah!"

Then, they were silent. They still walked, but faster now. He glanced at her. "Am I supposed to let you win?"

"Yesss!" she hollered, laughing, and took off down the street. I'm bookin'! she thought.

In two seconds flat, he was passing her by in long, easy strides. "Uh-unh, can't," he said, and gave her a loving look. "Victor . . . always wins."

Yes, sure, she was thinking you can outrun me because you're a guy. But any other way, I'm just as equal—Yes, I am!

Talley screeched with the giggles. Too dawn cool! No way was she going to pass him. But she stayed with him, clear to the bus stop, not *even* a pace behind him.